MAGELLAN 7

MAGELLAN 7

Richard Lauer

iUniverse, Inc.
Bloomington

MAGELLAN 7

iUniverse books may be ordered through booksellers or by contacting:

iUniverse
1663 Liberty Drive
Bloomington, IN 47403
www.iuniverse.com
1-800-Authors (1-800-288-4677)

ISBN: 978-1-4620-6663-6 (sc)
ISBN: 978-1-4620-6664-3 (ebk)

Printed in the United States of America

iUniverse rev. date: 11/07/2011

It is better to be generous than just.
It is sometimes better to sympathize instead to understand.

-Human Destiny

CHAPTER ONE

10 and Counting

I T'S IRONIC TO start at the end, but to tell you the truth, I really don't know where else to begin this odyssey from France back to my house in the United States. It was a little more than five years ago at the funeral for my best friend Joe Hatheridge, of the Boston Brahmin[1] Hatheridges, when the world I had known was suddenly and irrevocably changed forever. What sickened me most, however, was the horrible death Joe had endured at his mansion in West Palm. Not since my days at the FBI had I seen such psychopathic evil exacted upon a man's body. Although Joe's death was a blow to normalcy, complacency, and immortality, if only for another twenty-four hour grace period, it wasn't the only one that shook NASA's foundations that day. Two astronauts had also been killed just as brutally, only Campbell and Snyder weren't mission specialists or test pilots milling around Cape Canaveral. They were the Captain and Galactic Navigator for Magellan 7, the greatest ship in the history of space travel. Despite the three murders being tragedies on various levels, they couldn't be connected by motive anymore than physical evidence. The only thing the three crime scenes had in common, besides their gruesome bestiality, was all were void of clues of who, what, how, and more importantly, why.

There was nothing to initiate one criminal investigation, let alone link the three to a madman on the loose in South Beach.

With nothing to work with physically or circumstantially, it was impossible to draw conclusions much less a composite sketch of anyone of interest. Being invited by the FBI to assist in an advisory capacity due to my past record of successfully tracking serial killers, I was privy to all three crime scenes, particularly Joe's. But after three days, not even I could pick up a scent. That's to be expected after twenty years of having no direct correspondences "from Hell"[2] or from Minerva Keres, the Femme Fatale from Hell's Kitchen. My gut instincts, although kept honed in the pursuit of liars, cheats, and charlatans[3], were also drawing blanks.

Joe's six-foot drop left more than a gaping hole in St. John's Cemetery. We were not only best friends; we were colleagues, bloodhounds sniffing for that Right Stuff[4]. We were part of the quality control wing at NASA. Basically, whoever aspired to the stars had to first pass through our headhunters' gauntlet.

It wasn't easy coming to grips with Joe's sudden demise, and I was one of his pallbearers. I knew as I glared into the mortal abyss the NASA Home Office of Security and Clearance would never be the same. Holes in hearts are not very different from vacancies in 10x10 foot cubicles. Nothing could bridge that rent or plug that dike, not even a doubting finger of Thomas[6]. There was no solace, no closure, regardless of how many times I turned that other proverbial cheek. All that last spade full of dirt did was close one more chapter in a never-ending story that made absolutely no sense. To a well-seasoned bloodhound who was versed in the nuances of mixed signals and the stench of dying dreams, that was tantamount to trying to smell a dirty rat with a stuffy nose.

Everything was turned upside down. What else was to be expected when Science was more concerned about "raising the dead"[7] than keeping the living alive? I suppose it was no more maddening than Miami Dolphins football surpassing Jesus on Sunday depth charts. I knew I couldn't retreat to the sidelines. Not now. Not again. I had too much love and respect for Joe to ever allow my feelings and thoughts to be compromised by survivor guilt, of "better him than me."

On the morning following the ghastly murders, all three men shared the top billing of "it bleeds it leads." As days passed, however,

Joe was gradually exiled to the filler sections between the funnies and self-righteous editorials. Eventually, the headlines were monopolized by those flyboys, our emissaries to the stars. Don't get me wrong, NASA mourned Joe's passing, but ever so topically and briefly. It was in all likelihood a combination of envy and jealousy for his patrician[8] lineage. Being the privileged son of Industrial Tycoon Joseph Pennington Hatheridge IV didn't elicit much sympathy or ink. People didn't want to know about the life and death of an entitled elitist as much as they did their tragic heroes to the heavens.

Even as flags at half mast were unfolding, I was breaking down bits and pieces of raw material in my hind gut that not even my overactive imagination, with its reductions of the absurd, could explain, define, or level an incriminating finger at.

Was it possible? Was there a nexus beyond the transparency of NASA? How could I not inquire? When following your instincts, you invariably lead with your chin. That's another one of those drawbacks that portend all second-guesses to the contrary. Therein lied the gist of my peril; what brought three brilliant lives to a sudden, tragic halt on the same night in question? If they were worthless pieces of shit, I'd say good riddance. But they were good, solid men untainted by scandal and vicious innuendo. You could look high and low; they were still as clean as a newborn's conscience. They didn't even have a negative comment on their personnel files that dog a man for the remainder of his days. Norman Rockwell never portrayed men more idyllic and reminiscent of the Halcyon Days when wagers were friendly and addictions limited to ice cream, soda pop, and Bazooka Joe bubblegum.

I might not have had a dowager's intimates of lap dogs in heat in regards to Campbell and Snyder, but what I did know is Joe had no known enemies outside golf courses, racquetball courts, and auction houses. Those who knew Joe beyond a handshake and cup of coffee genuinely liked him. Once you got over the fact he was filthy rich, he was just a regular one-leg-in-the-pants-at-a-time guy, only he had very expensive tastes. All it takes though is one asshole that doesn't like you. That's all it ever takes to punch your ticket out of this dodge[11], one unhappy camper, one disgruntled employee, one jealous ex-lover. That's what makes the Reaper an even bigger prick to be talked about in locker rooms.

It was almost cliché to say Joe was decent and fair. He carefully weighed and measured his words before saying anything to anyone. It wasn't in that holier-than-thou sense of Right Wing nuts that proclaim to have the answer to every question. Granted, Joe may have ruffled flight feathers of would-be candidates, but that was part of our job as Agents to the Stars. Sure he could be a dogmatic, Iditarod[12] task master driving forth his pack but he was steadfast in his convictions and always by the book. He took a no frills, no thrills approach to tracking people and dates no longer found on tacky calendars. You would expect nothing less from a dedicated team leader.

Before my off-the-official-record investigation began, I was already auditioning speculations from water cooler sources. Ex-candidates recommended for the Sierra-Charlie[13] Club seemed a logical place to start. But would someone's dismissal from the Space Program render them homicidal? That's a big step to take on the ladder of conjecture. Between stages of denial and anger, I couldn't help but think what I was getting myself into. It's not that I was gun shy from being once bitten, it's just that I couldn't help but wonder what School of Hard Knocks would become my eventual Alma Mater.

Is burying our dead a wake up call or simply a call to arms? I suppose, in retrospect, my revenge was fueled by a mid-life crisis for one last great and epic hunt. So much was boiling in a moment's rage of here and gone into the vapors of Eternity. Everybody's life inevitably becomes a blip in the obituaries. Where else can seventy to seventy-five years be capsulated for daily consumption? It's all so very nice and tidy to have life summed up in a few brief sentences between storks and swirling vultures[14] with live feeds at five, six and ten o'clock. For better or worse, everything's condensed in format. Man's mind only follows in the steps of transistors, computer chips, and compact discs. It's easier to grab life by the horns that way. It's also easier to understand something when you can stick it in your hip pocket. Knowing what we want is just our consolation for not knowing who we are in the Big Picture. That's why man is so unique, for he's the only animal who desires to not only be seen and heard, but smelt on a daily basis.

Perhaps the illusion isn't in the attraction, but in us? What else is available in maelstroms of dark victories and bittersweet surrenders but more shadings of self-absorbed milkmaids with their one in, one out entitlement psychosis? I learned long ago that digging didn't guarantee treasures any more than answers beyond the grave. What I was able to ascertain after three days of soul searching however was pretty much the same rehashed bullshit released for public dissemination under the voyeuristic First Amendment. But nobody from Langley to Miami had anything to further add to the criminal discourse of person or persons unknown. The three homicides were so unique that master profilers at the F.B.I. Behavioral Science Unit had no working model for this new type of slaughter and postal rage.

I could accept one crime scene being clean and cold to the touch, but three! That was unheard of in investigative circles. No killer was that good or lucky, especially on the same night. The bloodbaths were free of even a whisper of Charlotte Corday[15]. With so much carnage, you'd expect a little cross-pollination and carry over of mitochondrial DNA[16]. But there was nothing, absolutely nothing. Forensic scientists at Quantico[17] said the crime scenes were so pristine that, if not for their apparent barbarity, they would have been considered suicides. No hair samples, clothing fibers, fingerprints, or bodily fluids. There were also no signs of forced entry at any of the crime scenes.

It was primarily for that reason I believed Joe was surprised by this man upon returning home that night from O'Brien's Bar and Grill. Don't get me wrong, a woman can certainly kill a man, but her ways are generally subtle, methodical, a Chinese water torture of the soul. Besides, the Chief Coroner out of Broward stated Joe was instantly killed by blunt force trauma before being decapitated. To this day, it still troubles me to say that. Dirt, as you very well know, only buries bones, nothing more.

Regardless of how many spooked strays I cut, there was still yet another to test the flanks of my "been there, done that" soliloquy. I was the only one who believed Joe's murder wasn't a random act.

I couldn't accept his death being a freak incident because he was the only one beheaded. To me, Joe's death seemed personal, almost vindictive in a way, as if it was symbolic of something.—But what? How do you rationalize, interpret, or even begin to explain a man's tongue shoved up his ass? What kind of message was that? And whom was it intended for? All it had to have meaning to, though, was the twisted, deranged killer, and he wasn't talking—at least not yet.

I knew in every homicide investigation time meant nothing and timing meant everything. Someone somewhere had to have knowledge of this maniac. Crimes of this barbaric nature always got somebody talking. But would it be the taunting killer? Would he reveal his warped mind and motive like the Zodiac Killer[18]? Something so big would surely have somebody laying claim to it; it almost went without saying. After all, no ego-maniac ever wants to leave his works unsigned.

I couldn't wait for the cops or some Judas to betray a dark disturbing secret. It wasn't my style. I was always proactive, whether I was tracking killers or space cadets. You could find me in a million places, but never the Devil's workshop[19].

At the time, I still believed good things happened to good people. It's the standard refrain in all karmic circles. But where was Justice, that blind bitch, now? Before the last speck of dust settled over that depth charge[20] to Eternity, I knew I had to maintain objectivity. Distance and indifference are the cornerstones of deductive reasoning. Any field agent will tell you, if personal feelings seep into an investigation it will be flawed and compromised. I was very cognizant of this, almost to the point of being too self-conscious. As time went on, my emotions weren't so much steeled over as benumbed by a morbid redundancy of playing Joe's crime scene over and over again in my head. Eventually I once more became the cold critic assessing style points and criminal methodology. What I'd be searching for was the intentional and the accidental. I should point out that Joe's blood wasn't just splashed on the walls; it was painted with strokes of genius by this master of disguise.

Joe's proclivities, you ask? Why, the man was good as his word, and not only during those ritual forays attended on Sundays. His

Joneses could easily be vouched for and readily dismissed. After twenty years, I could say without bias that Joe was pathetic when it came to getting down and dirty. To him, a sleazy Stop and Sock motel was the Hyatt Regency. His peccadilloes were also so insignificant they were dead ends in themselves. He didn't smoke, gamble or take drugs, legally or recreationally, if you know what I mean. But that's how life is, different turn-ons, different hard-ons. It's said what you gravitate toward is what influences you in and out of bed. It was only after Janet's death two years earlier when Joe fell off that one glass of Chivas[21] wagon. Such things are to be expected, however. Watching a loved one get eaten by cancer is the most painful disappearing act for any loyal husband or loving son.

I envied Joe's marriage to Janet more than his wealth. The downstairs sofa was never an alternative or ultimatum in his house. They had everything and each other. With them, "happily ever after" was no blatant abomination. They were living proof that sperm and monogamy could co-exist outside fantasyland.

Joe wasn't like most people who picked their poisons and battles as they did their noses. His was a higher road to a higher calling. Everything about him was on the up and up. Even his contingent of bluebloods came from sturdy New England trees that no more threw shade than they did shady people. He was rather fundamental in his singularity, having but one face for all occasions. How are such things possible? Wasn't everyone fractured and faceted? But despite having the same face and same act it never got tired; it really didn't.

Joe wasn't a skirt chaser either. To him, that was just one boob in pursuit of two others. It was poetic rectitude without doggerel[22] verses and bastardized editions of misogynist's[23] monthly. He wasn't a switch hitter[24] either. He was upfront and candid about his horizontal preferences without protesting a bit too much. Joe might have spoken fluent French, but when it came to ménage a trios[25], his tongue stuck to the roof of his mouth as if coated in a party of peanut butter, molasses, and Elmer's glue! In that swinging sense, Joe was the epitome of Perry Como and vanilla ice cream.

Hopeless romantics are a special breed, there's no doubt about it. Understanding Heaven and Hell is predicated upon your knowledge of she wolves and how blind you really are when in love for the first, last and only time. With Joe there were no ifs, ands, or "butt buddies." So I could cross off jealous and jilted lovers as possible suspects. That was another no-brainer, just like bookies and drug dealers who also tried to cover their tracks in the snows of Hail Columbia[26].

Practicing what's preached before a dewy-eyed choir is only refreshing when kept in proper perspective. A parachute might very well be a good idea unless, of course, you're the pilot in the cockpit—then it takes on a whole other meaning. Being a stand-up guy isn't necessarily skewed because you kneel in church.

Joe was too Ivyized[27] to be narrow-minded and bigoted. That was another endearing trait about him; he was flexible even on those hot-button issues that tended for the most part to list just to the left of center. Not only was he liberal minded, he was a mental sponge, absorbing every last feature regardless how arcane, obscure, or trivial. Joe didn't just have an eye for detail, he had an eagle eye.

Joe's hobbies, which I knew but never quite understood, were limited to auction houses and surfing websites for rare and valuable antiques. His love of flying was only surpassed by his obsession with collecting old things from worlds long since forgotten. Sculptures, etchings, paintings, busts, and last but not least, books—rare and unusual books. Joe's inherent wealth allowed him these indulgences from Sotheby's to Christie's[28]. In thirty years, Joe had amassed not just a treasure trove, but a museum that spanned the centuries and Muses.

With Joe, there were no scavenger hunts in bargain basements or smelly garages. Everything he purchased was top notch and first rate. Joe believed only in the best and finest no matter the price. He was anal that way. But like he always said, "you get what you pay for."

What was equally baffling was Joe's computer had been hacked into by his killer.—But why? There was nothing sensitive or vital to National Security. The files and records were all unclassified documents. That's what made this so problematic, why didn't the killer just take the disc. Let's be serious for a moment. You just don't murder and mutilate a man then have reservations about taking something that doesn't belong to you. Shit like that just doesn't happen. Assailants never stop to think about robbery charges after committing a capital offense. Yet in spite of my input, those pinheads at the Miami Bureau insisted it was a virus similar to the cyber terrorist Michelangelo[29]. I couldn't buy into that reasoning. For one thing it was too convenient, and secondly, the deletions weren't pervasive throughout the user files and program.

I couldn't discount the possibility of the omissions being a cover up or red herring. Compared to some of the other asinine theories circulating around NASA it really didn't sound all that absurd or far-fetched. It's not that I knew better, it's just that I knew differently, and sometimes that makes all the difference in the world.

The killer wasn't taking any unnecessary chances with excess baggage. Somewhere out there was one less loose thread for the killer to worry about being pulled as a finger in a sophomoric prank. This killer was not only thorough, he was highly intelligent. He was mad but not crazy, likable but not friendly, young but not that young, and oh yes, white—white as a neo-con[30] out of Wyoming. This guy wasn't just going to spill his guts out as a pregnant piñata at a stick wielding debutante's coming out party. This killer needed no lackeys to feed his ego. It's not that he was devoid of vanity; it's just that he had priorities beyond the pond's reflection[31]. He was no ordinary killer, if one can be so ascribed. By the looks of it he wasn't a work in progress either. He was a finished product of some underworld finishing school where they teach Windsor knots on Colombian neckties[32].

When I was at the Bureau, I tried to envision perps before seeing the sketch artist's final draft. MO's at crime scenes said more than just methods of dispatch from this world to the next. I found you could no more separate a man from his actions than you could the actions from the man. Young investigators forget psychic prints are left behind at crime scenes too. But because these unconventionalities fly below the forensic radar they are downplayed and relegated to poppycock.

This killer presented many dichotomies. Oddly, they remained in balance even when substance became shadow and man an animal again. It was almost as if there was a method to his madness. Still, I couldn't get a read on this guy. Maybe it's true, "if you don't use it, you lose it." I wouldn't necessarily subscribe to that across the board, but it does have merit. My situation, however, was unique because I was in voluntary seclusion in paradise more so than forced retirement and death by a thousand budget cuts.

Campbell and Snyder were molded just like Joe—square and clean. Neither had ties to organized crime. Such seedy associations ran counter to everything they strived not to be, or for that matter, be seen with. The only connection they had to each other is they worked for NASA. Other than that, there were no social circles overlapping. Neither of them knew Joe on a personal basis either. Their crime scenes were equally disturbing, only they, like I said, were not decapitated, nor were their computers tampered with. Pundits and other talking heads[33] stoked the coals of fear by claiming a serial killer was targeting NASA. It was no secret that at any given time, several mass-murderers were working the Country with their traveling magic shows so the possibility, even on that perverse level, existed to keep those options open for further review.

Despite the potential for real and make believe killers on the war path, I knew the field of suspects would soon be narrowed and whittled down just as those fidgety little brats who understood nothing whatsoever of life or death, but were in remedial attendance nonetheless, as if this initiation into Eternity would somehow or another recruit them into that bigger circle jerk of here today and gone tomorrow. My years as an FBI special agent out of New York at least gave my fledgling hobby horse some much needed legs to stand on, only I wouldn't have a golden Aegis[34] to protect me and ward off evil.

Joe's death infused me with more than black coffee with lots of sugar. All I know is I felt alive again. And I hadn't felt like that since before I lost my eye during a hunting expedition in Lower Manhattan. Such was my consolation, to get the right girl but lose my left eye.

How could I refuse to throw my hat into the ring? I was tired of being associated with a tender mouse[35] and a cushy desk job at NASA. Sure I had reservations and doubts, but what sane man doesn't? My self-imposed exile was far removed from the streets of New York and Minerva Keres, the Dark Mistress who ate her victim's eyes on the half shell.

What I wouldn't have given to be twenty years younger and the Special Agent in charge of that newly formed task force out of Miami. To always have a new view and a fresh scent would be so different from sloppy seconds and stale leftovers from the Trojan[36] night before. Secondary investigators orbiting the periphery never have any contingency plans. What, after all, is the alternative to lead sled dog? It's only a natural chain of command reaction as taking lunch orders, riding bitch, and finger printing low-lives loitering the halls of the Sixth Circuit Court.

Don't forget, wishful thinking is just another consequence of growing long in the tooth.

The who, and the why, was a never-ending merry-go-round. As you're well aware, there are as many ways to kill a man, as there are reasons to put him in the ground. Sometimes it's simply someone who can't stand the fact that somebody else is living good while being good for nothing. It takes all kinds to round out any field. Some kill to settle old scores that only exist on their warped scoreboard. Those diabolical killers, which include the Unabomber[37] and Minerva Keres, are sly, crafty, and frighteningly intelligent. Minerva Keres had an IQ that would put to shame any past or present member of MENSA[38]. That's what makes these elite killers so dangerous. They can go anywhere and function like the guy next door, or they can hide in the wide open without arousing suspicion.

Why does death enamor us to the good in people? Is it due to not speaking ill of the dead? Death does tend to keep alive that illusion, even after the eulogy is over with its Our Fathers and Hail Mary's into the end zone. Good, bad, or indifferent, I still couldn't allow Joe to become just another faceless victim who passes into the oblivion of a government statistic without so much as a favorable word to mark his transformation from fleeting man to fleeting memory.

Even before Joe was cold in the ground, the head honchos at NASA wrote him off as a bad expense. All those bean counters were concerned about was safeguarding the surviving member of Magellan 7, Commander Thomas Webster. A twenty-four hour security detail had been assigned to ensure his safety. National Treasures in orange jumpsuits were too precious of a public relations commodity to lose. Let me remind you that Commander Webster wasn't just any astronaut; he was the very face of NASA, the front man in every ticker-tape parade down Fifth Avenue. NASA wasn't about to lose their Science Officer for Magellan 7 any more than scrub their precious mission—not with a launch date T—Minus ten days and counting. This time frame had to be honored. It was imperative for that was when the gas giants, Jupiter and Saturn, with their powerful gravitational fields would be at their furthest distances from Earth, a window that wouldn't open and present itself again for another 157.6 years. Besides, it was easier to replace two astronauts than three with those backups waiting in the wings for their turn to prove they had what it took to join that exclusive club as something other than weightless understudies chomping at the oxygen bit.

I couldn't help but beat myself up. I had become the consummate masochist overnight. Who's to say things would have turned out differently if I had hooked up with Joe at O'Brien's Bar and Grill that night? Destiny can no more be changed than a Southern Baptist who believes in religious cookbooks[39] and bribery through nightly prayer.

Still, I couldn't help but think about alternative outcomes and scenarios. The day of Joe's funeral thankfully slinked away with a skittish afternoon bleeding into evening as a Boston liberal on a microphone studded soapbox. Since I was the first to arrive, it seemed only fitting I should be the last to depart this Empire of Granite that had no mutual ground for the living to stand upon. It, however, was just another vacancy that couldn't be filled, like an empty orchestra[40] that has no emergency funds for a second fiddle.

CHAPTER TWO

9th Avenue

S OON, I JOINED that vehicular procession scattering as so much stardust along 9th Avenue. Despite surroundings gradually becoming more familiar, things were still far from being considered normal and A-OK. Known things are deceiving like that, just like candy or anything else sugar coated that creates cavities that cannot be filled with silver, gold, or mercury. Returning home, as any circular obligation, is part of our geometric holding pattern. Plots[41], as plotting courses, are all about getting back to one's roots. But getting back to Square One only retraces the bumper-to-bumper morning grind of being sold down Time's River, only instead of backwards a wage slave puts it into overdrive as if that added extra feature were a change of pace rather than a surface variation of a show room theme.

What, after all, is the meaning of shapes and images that suggestively flow unchecked? Is man not also another mutable component in this interchangeable loop of scapegoats and fall guys? Or is he just one more insufferable fool in a long line of Washington outsiders forever looking into the breach? Habits, good and bad, are a form of indentured servitude. That's the common bond linking these two Johns together with that one revelation about the light at the end of the tunnel. The ambivalence of uncertainty is manifest in every venture that truly seeks to get to the bottom of something, however dark and disturbing. Organized crime, as organized religion, only incorporated its own God-fatherly version and take on horse races, flood stories, and little green men from Outer Space. Still, doubt nags even the most ardent supporters of additional elbow room.

Thoughts, marginal and over-the-top, which I hadn't entertained in years, were front and center again, along with those shifty eyed whores who had more tricks than a scheming sphinx with her deranged countdown of four to two to three[42]. Maybe it's true after all—maybe that elusive sixth sense comes with that impending sixth foot? Who knows, maybe death is nothing more than a reverse confirmation process of man's birth into eternity? Still, it doesn't quite explain how lovers can drown in the Sea of Love when they were once fish that found evolutionary pay dirt at the end of a fallopian tube.

My practical bent no longer did genuflect or take bread in any compressed, waferized form. My savior was my work in which I buried myself alive every Monday through Friday. Beyond that salaried threshold everything else was secondary, including my sex life, which had been reduced to grainy skin flicks, chance encounters, and chat rooms with faceless strangers with alluring aliases.

I must admit, even when I was married to Karen, I never had plumy visions of little white houses with thirty year nuts that would envy loan sharks from the Bowery[43]. That family man clock stopped ticking so long ago it was no longer right twice a day, let alone once in a lifetime. Besides, kids were nothing more than known accomplices who took a man hostage in his own goddamn house.

You have to be realistic about hard-ons in regards round holes and round pegs. Over the years, I sounded one too many Potemkin[44] pasts to not be suspicious of three ring circuses that start with engagements and end in all-out custody battles over everything under the Sun, including rug rats. In my defense it's easy to mistake cellmates for soul mates when you're young, dumb, and full of cum. Eventually, however, everything comes to light whether a man wants to accept it or not. It took me twelve years before I regained my faculties. Having not one, but two hard heads will do that to a man. No man is immune or free from the lash of the pussy's whip. In that sense we're all masochists. Eve is not symbolic of man's fall from Paradise by accident you know.

If I learned one thing from my marital ordeal, besides not playing with balls and chains, it's that freedom is much too precious to waste. Compromise only means doing something you didn't want to do in the first place. Give-and-take is never about happiness as it is keeping the peace. That's all tit-for-tat is, a bargainer's delight, a fool's game. To me life's too short to be settling for half the kitty. You have to remember we only have one chance to make this right. There's no coming back, no return policy after three days of bait and switch. This is it; it's a one-shot deal. That's all it ever was, and that's all it will ever be. Religious nuts can say what they want about Jesus and life after death, but we made God in our image, albeit without the hooked nose and swarthy complexion. No other creature manufactures God or has need to. That is man's knock, his evolutionary shortcoming, to not only be the king of beasts but the king of kings.

My entire existence at NASA had been relegated to being a suited spoke in a well-greased wheel so big and impersonal that I couldn't feel it turn even when it crushed dreams and pulverized candidates as an out-of-control juggernaut. Prior to Joe's death, I was, if not happy with the arrangement, than at least satisfied with the long hours and short vacations. I must confess it was therapeutic and somewhat refreshing. Instead of looking for rotten, no good sons of bitches, I was searching for good, honest men. Sure it was a glorified talent contest, but I was one of the judges and coordinators who had the power to approve or deny access and entry to the next graduated level. In many ways, it was an erotic act, as it generally is when screwing someone, the only difference being there were no cigarettes, saliva, or phone numbers being swapped and mutually exchanged.

Background checks were my specialty more so than those uncomfortable face-to-face interviews with nervous candidates who couldn't help but stare at my black eye patch. Nobody could compete with me when it came to tracking candidates on paper trails, except, perhaps, Joe. I rather fashioned myself a biographical archaeologist in pursuit of dirty laundry and skeletal remains in closets. I enjoyed the hunt as much as the dig. After all, a man is the sum of all the parts he's ever played, and everything he was or was ever going to be was found there, regardless how fatal, monstrous, or benign. I tried to look at man's past as a leviathan prowling the subconscious depths, one I had to approach from various angles before harpooning it and reeling it in as some Chesapeake catch of the day. I was as Ahab, only I was in pursuit of the Lie, the Great White Lie, and of bringing it back to the surface.

Since childhood I had been obsessed with hide and seek. You might say I was addicted the first time I was baptized and christened "it." But I liked being "it." I preferred to be the one everyone was running from. It held power and prestige. Besides, I liked to see where people hid. You can tell a lot about a man from his hiding place. This fascination was what spurred me on to the FBI Academy and eventually New York City, where only the best of the best performed and then hid on and off Broadway. My days at the Bureau gave me a greater appreciation for this innate sense that even transcended Electronic Domains and closets. This special talent of hearing what a candidate was saying long after they stopped talking about themselves was not so much a process of elimination as it was a culmination of childhood events, of not only throwing rocks, but looking under them.

In a perverse way, I found it exhilarating to walk in someone else's dirty moccasins. What better way to see aspirants before their formal interviews? Cross-referencing employment histories, credit reports, and military records made me an expert on other people's lives. I actually knew some candidates who entered my web better than they knew or wanted to know themselves. "For official use only" allowed for these absurdities to co-exist with trick questions and two-way mirrors. But working for the Man, whose symbol is the Washington Monument, afforded me this carte blanche to pillage and loot all available data banks.

After all, my job was about promoting and projecting a clean-cut American image. Why else do you suppose rocket ships are milky white and phallic shaped?

Yet who passed and failed was no hocus pocus accomplished by scrying[45] crystal balls. It was just one more Department of Defense statute that had long ago calcified into a standard operating procedure in every NASA training manual. I didn't make the rules or set the criteria for wannabes with the Right Stuff. I was just following orders sent down by men on Capitol Hill, men who I would no more meet in this life than I would the next. But it begged the question: did NASA set unrealistically high standards or just more experimental ten pins willing to risk their lives for a chance at the ride of a lifetime?

Tests were designed—more like rigged—to deny access to nine out of every ten applicants who walked through the front door. Formal grillings only afforded us at quality control that much more latitude in discouraging as many as we ensnared with our honesty test that utilized north, south, east and west as more than cardinal points on a man's inner compass. Throughout the years, I had heard just about everything. Some stories were airtight while others reeked to the high heavens of Icarus, John Glenn, and post-Sputnik boom. Forget about kitchen sinks and shooting matches. I've known candidates to lie about everything from their disposable incomes to the size of their cojones[46]. But to catch a liar and separate him from his well-rehearsed story was a lot easier in theory than practice. When all you know about someone is stored on a computer disc, you are immediately at a strict disadvantage. X-factors only added to the equation of who these candidates really were beyond a name, rank, and Social Security number.

I have to admit it wasn't easy tripping up candidates. Dislodging them from their illusions of grandeur was a Herculean labor. Good salesmen are just as adept at selling you a bag of shit, as they are a bottle of Shinola. Naturally, little lies were the hardest things to detect because they were like a colorless, odorless gas approaching critical mass. Still I found the genealogy of every whopper and tall tale told to me. Don't get me wrong; I enjoy a good story just as much as the next man. I could tolerate an honest mistake too, as long as it wasn't held hostage by sociopathic tendencies that forever sees one in every idiosyncratic countdown and launch sequence of events that throws the baby out with the bath water.

By their very nature, judgments are subjective, arbitrary things found somewhere between Star Chambers[47] and Kangaroo Courts[48]. At NASA it wasn't just about the truth, but if you could be trusted with the most expensive toys ever invented by man.—One man—One decision. How's that for reducing Papal Bulls to bullion? But that's how it was before Progress prompted change to lynch laws and hemp parties[49]. Such is the travesty of liberal courts, to allow convicted killers to die of old age on Death Row. That, though, is modern man in a nutshell; fixing things that aren't broken. Change for the sake of change is nothing more than vanity run amok. How else do you explain gaudy skyscrapers prohibiting ancient light[50] in the name of urban renewal?

As you know, history can be retold, but it's not supposed to be rewritten. Oh sure, Kotex brigades[51] and racial extortionists can put their own choreographed spin on wages, hiring practices and glass ceilings, but all they're creating is just another Frankenstein monster who's afraid of fire. Sure there are obvious holes in that white noise, and not just from Rusty Nails and Roman Spears[52]. What we see and what we believe we see are so radically opposed that the two versions can't be reconciled or considered as being in the same burning bush league.

Is this all fashioned by mere chance or are we just fatalistically predisposed to take a bullet before a knee? As for myself, I lost that taste for fish tales after my parents' premature death from cancer when I was a kid growing up in St. Louis, where another kind of bird ruled the roost atop flagpoles. But if life is predestined, trying to change anything, including us, is not only futile, it's stupid. Quite frankly, it would make more sense taking a supermodel to an all-you-can-eat buffet. As a working concept, however, it did pester me long enough to keep me second guessing when I hedged on Sundays with Free Will and good luck charms, those fetishes of Third World countries that only knew Almighty Buck as an animalistic currency of Pig Latin and Pidgin English.

Seriously, when you think about it, what God would want to be worshiped by bigots, terrorists, and fanatics? Over time, such things tend to answer themselves if you're open to the suggestion that there is nothing beyond the threshold of death except grave robbers and night crawlers. But where, you ask, is the redeemer of lost causes in this win, place and show me where the inheritance money is going?

But for all Man's breakthroughs, evolution is still the monkey wrench[53] in the creationist's ten speed gears[54]. The two can no more be reconciled than great apes to Mitered Primates[55]. That's another sore spot that will never scab and heal over. Pompous theists want no connection to Darwinian knuckle scrapers in the African mist. Uncle Sam is as far a distant relative that many are ready and willing to go. After all, what's self-denial but slipping a mickey to yourself? The only problem is that those side effects never wear off. That, however, is man's inconsistency, to be a lover of life who abhors mercy killings and slaughter rules.

Nothing could stop that hemorrhage cascading down from a cluttered attic where memories collected dust as donations to a shadowy past that years before ended its own Galanty show[56] in the land of the living and still in Saturday night demand. It was slow suicide at rush hour, oxymoronic companion to jumbo shrimp, military intelligence, and compassionate conservatism. Herd mentalities only elevated jumping to conclusions to the throne room of lemmings. Even traffic lights changed colors as chameleons with their own trickle down economics of an inch of concrete here and a lot of assholes over there.

My house had also become a place of conformity through osmosis, existing only as a familiar setting to eat, sleep, shit, shower, and shave. The bricks weren't quite yet mine either. There was still the matter of another note for ten years. It was a motivation that, although not exactly ground breaking, was nonetheless instrumental in getting my hairy ass out of bed every morning. Still, I wasn't sure if death was all that scary or if it just had a bad press agent. Maybe life's the game with birth and death the start and finish lines? For all we know, death can be just like when a battery runs out of juice inside a child's toy. It could very well be possible that dead men aren't supposed to tell tales or anything else for that matter. Maybe the end was the end of everything a man was or was ever going to be, and after this three-dimensional plane there were no other flights to catch. In reality, that sudden stop after ideally speaking, there are only temporary winners and permanent losers. There is no in between, no draw to make things equal and commensurate. The same can be said about playing fields that are prejudicially tilted to the uniformed talents of the home team. That chalked truth can no more be concealed and covered up than a boxcar named Bertha. This acceptable cheating held sway wherever man stood, knelt, buckled under, or otherwise redefined himself in seedy convenience store checkout lines at four in the morning

How could I not feel swindled? Lonely lunches would now precede junkets of Chinese take-out that made every entrée taste like cardboard and yellow dye 23. Only over that cavernous social gap there were no flowers, wreathes, or granite testimonials. Scored memories were all that remained as confirmation for Court 14 at eight o'clock sharp every Saturday morning.

There's no consolation in the knowledge of every man being expendable. We're all replaceable in time, grade, and assigned parking space. That's the way it is with any bureaucracy; the music continues to play even after all the chairs are removed. But whereas NASA had suitable replacements fresh off the academy's assembly line, there were no such cookie cut descendents of Whitney[57] to fill Joe's size 12's. At that time in my life, a loss wasn't supposed to eclipse the last man standing, yet somehow or another it did just that. I couldn't help but be fixated, not only with that opening on my dance card, but the big 5-0. It sounded so adult, so grown up. It was my entire existence, my whole frame of reference from as far back as I could remember, to everything I wanted to now conveniently forget.

Everything was crammed and contracted. All the baggage, all the baggage handlers, and all those ignorant assholes that thought they owned the road with their gas guzzling lead sleds that made some Arab prick rich with every fill up of regular or supreme.

But I could no more change myself than change lanes. I was too set in my bachelor ways to alter outcomes on Valentine's Day. Bonding, cuddling, sharing, and looking for things in common on a Chicago deep dish pizza was too radical a departure to embark upon especially when my mind was already made up in regards to politics, religion, and god forbid, mother-in-laws!

Sure, getting a dog as a companion was an option. Those repetitive training sessions could, if one was not careful, blur the leash law between who was actually Pavlov's pet project when the doorbell rang. Besides, superiority complexes are generally reserved for the young and callow. When you have several decades to squander on expensive women and cheap sex, it's a lot different than having one, possibly two remaining before false teeth, arthritis, and swollen prostates manifest themselves at ammonia scented nursing homes.

Of course there was always networking, but that was a tool of social climbers on corporate ladders just as wonder bras, K-Y jelly, and power lunches, where dry martinis and dry humor could accompany one another without fear of being seen together in public. What, though, was a single tick on grandfather or cuckoo clocks? Was it also something seeking ad hoc[58] immortality with the drinking of a host's precious blood? Maybe at the end of the day we all have to learn to think outside the box before we can ever peacefully get into one. Who knows? Crazier things have been known to happen.

CHAPTER THREE

The 8th Wonder of the World

I HATE TO SOUND so presumptuous, but a brief overview of Magellan 7 is necessary at this time. Five years may not seem like a long time in the grand scheme of things but in the mainstream media with its never-ending flow of current events, five years may as well be five million.

The NASA Review Board, a select governing committee that had a very public name but a very private face, announced the promotion of Henry Collins and Richard Sanders to replace Captain Campbell and Galactic Navigator Snyder aboard Magellan 7 the following morning. It was a sound choice, one that went down easily without a shot of bitters. I believed one, if not both astronauts, should have been originally slated to join Commander Webster aboard Magellan 7. After all, I did the preliminary grunt work on Richard Sanders in 2010 before he was highly recommended for candidate certification and Academy placement by Joe. I recall our collective shock when he wasn't initially elevated to Alpha Team. I wasn't familiar with Henry Collins's resume as much, but what was bandied about him at NASA was limited to the glowing, amazing and spectacular. His glaring omission from Alpha Team left many pondering and scratching their collective head. But at NASA, or anywhere else where people congregate to make and break bread, politics is predominant. NASA, being a government spawn, was always more about who you knew than what you knew. You can change professions but man will always be the same. That's just how it is anytime you put three or more people together in a room.

It's not as if a wrong was finally made right, it's just that the universal order of things was restored. Ironically, just like Thomas Webster, Henry Collins and Richard Sanders were also orphans, only from Detroit and Chicago respectively. The media outlets across America had a perpetual field day with this "I'll be damned" coincidence. Not only that, but their made-for-TV names just so effortlessly rolled off the tongue. It was Tom, Dick and Harry this, Tom, Dick and Harry that. Overnight they had morphed into every man for every body.

They were the latest media darlings who could say or do no wrong. They also became the envy and toast of every lunch bucket Louie who ever wanted to go some place special without any strings attached to his balls. Tom, Dick and Harry were suddenly the hottest ticket in every town from Bangor to Honolulu. But the truly remarkable thing about all this hoopla is they were heralded a success story before the ending was known in its entirety. And although everyone rooted for them and welcomed them into their hearts and homes, no one could actually lay claim to them as a long lost lottery stub.

Being foundlings raised in orphanages left numerous vacancies around holiday tables and family scrapbooks, where the remains of the dead lived on in absentia and Kodak moments. No one was particularly concerned about the Dickensian[59] details of their rough and tragic childhoods. The nation was too caught up in the raw, frenzied spectacle of the "Here and Now" to get carried away by water under the Bridge of Whys, of why three infants were abandoned after birth by their unknown mothers. Besides, Americans didn't care where a man was from as much as where he was going.

By a twist of fate, national treasures had to also be buried before they could be found. It was the feel good story of the year that came right on the heels of the Nation mourning the loss of Campbell and Snyder. Talk about a hundred and eighty degree turn and mood swing. Reporters occasionally dredged their youths in those emotionally charged wastelands that had no happy endings before the age of consent. By and large, stories were done tastefully, and more importantly, sympathetically. After all, nobody wanted to piss on Tom, Dick and Harry's parade. I mean, how could you beat up underdogs raised on a tougher love that reserved leather straps for more than designer britches? That was primarily the catalyst for this kid glove treatment. Every question was underhanded. There were no curve balls or royalties from "chin music" [60]. The answers they supplied were simple and straightforward as well. This held true whether individually wrapped or bundled together as a Trinity.

Tom, Dick and Harry were swiftly relegated to a different red-carpeted category of national celebrity, one that would inevitably take their rising star to the next level of Hollywood Headliner. Everyone in America was now along for the historic ride where man had never been before, and upon dark horses who came out of nowhere.

It was impossible to find fault with any of them. They were that special, that unique, that irresistible. They were always surrounded by a flink[61] of admirers swooning for 9 x 11 autographed glossies. It was indeed a media circus; only they were the main attraction. In addition to these public relation bonuses, Tom, Dick and Harry were also single, white males, which although not a prerequisite for becoming a Deep Space Ranger, was nonetheless looked favorably upon by NASA. Since 2011, with the online placement of permanently manned docking stations that stretched from the lunar colonies to within twenty thousand miles of Mars, came space tours of duty lasting anywhere from eighteen to thirty-six months. The importance of these missions and delicate exercises were never to be compromised by love triangles or other head masters. Simply put, there were to be no conflict of interests. Sober, even keeled demeanors were traits deemed desirable by NASA, which, truth be told, only wanted their boys in love with one thing: the mission.

Despite modern ships obtaining speeds far greater than in the early days of space travel, when Pioneer 10, launched in 1977, took thirty-one years to travel beyond the Kuiper Belt[62], it still required serious blocks of time to push scientific envelopes that had neither permanent ZIP codes nor e-mail addresses.

NASA, like Space, is a cold calculating business and just as numbing to the senses with its algebraic numbers and binary sequences of one and zero. Experiments are conducted at times just to see how the human body will perform under prolonged weightless conditions. How else is NASA to push daisies, boil blood, and give doctoral credence to their computer models? Human guinea pigs have to verify and substantiate their hypothetical conclusions if for nothing else to remove monkeys from their equations and chariots of fire.

Science isn't an exact science. Often times it's little more than a voluntary crapshoot, a donnybrook[63], if you will. The only difference, man is fighting his own prejudices and ignorance's while shedding his sacrificial blood throughout the Houses of the Zodiac.

However, if there was one ostensible box in which to store all the hopes of NASA it was in the reputed 8th Wonder of the World, Magellan 7. The Magellan Class had succeeded the Orion Shuttle Series as NASA's primary workhorse. The Magellan Class did it all, and without glitches or gremlins gumming up the works. Positioning and repairing deep space telescopes and conducting electromagnetic frequency tests were just some of their many assignments. Magellan 7 was the latest breakthrough in this highly evolved Super Order that revolutionized space travel. It also finally put to rest those five words Mission Control dreaded most, "Houston we have a problem".

Magellan 7 was hailed twice as fast, twice as big, and ten times more advanced and sophisticated than its previous predecessor, Magellan 6. It had sixteen plutonium booster rockets, five hydroponic gardens to ward off scurvy, twenty-one solar powered filtration systems that could convert sweat, urine, and all other hydrogen-based molecules into drinking water, one thousand one hundred forty-eight super computers that could calculate four hundred trillion problems a nanosecond, and eight storage pantries that could theoretically sustain a three man crew a thousand years without once resorting to rationing, pilfering or drawing straws.

Magellan 7 had to be something special; great journeys traditionally required great ships. They went hand-in-hand, just as those NASA scientists and engineers who created this technological marvel seated in the pantheon of those other pay—loaded gods of

Roman myth. Magellan 7's chief architect, by the way, was none other than Thomas Webster. Not only was this remarkable man the face of NASA, he was also one of its crafty wizards lurking behind the curtains. If you had never physically experienced Magellan 7, you will die with at least one more regret. Even to be cast in its shadow was an honor and privilege one would not soon forget.

Nothing invented ever had more gadgets, moving parts or computers. It was far and away the most magnificent, awe-inspiring ship ever created, not only by NASA, but Mankind. Magellan 7 was also the most expensive ship, costing eight-hundred and fifty billion dollars. You couldn't help but be dwarfed in its lordly presence. Even on Earth, it had a kind of heavenly aura surrounding it. How could it not? This behemoth was the equivalent of a thirty-six story building; only one that had fuel cells with a lift thrust capacity of three trillion horses. That's why people were overcome with anticipation. Nothing ever existed like Magellan 7, which only added to its totem luster and shine on Launch Pad 29.

Magellan 7 was designed exclusively for deep space travel. Its mission was to exceed the Terminator Shock[64] and unleash its army of scientific probes into the Coalsack[65] of the Southern Cross[66] where NASA had been receiving sophisticated radio waves since Camelot[67] in the summer of '63. This objective was to be accomplished in ten years, two hours and forty-seven seconds from time of ignition and take off at Cape Canaveral to Magellan 7's scheduled return to Earth in September 2030.

We at NASA were mesmerized and seized by the culmination of Mercury, Gemini, Friendship, Saturn, Viking, Apollo, and countless years of planning an escape velocity from this Devil's Island isolated in the Milky Way. This seminal event would change more than our history. It also gave every American a sense of accomplishment, of witnessing something their grandfathers never did.

In the recesses of my mind between half empty and half full I still couldn't help but channel that skeptic to counter balance this pandemonic glee.

What if this ten year mission was a waste of time and money, the two most precious commodities at NASA?

What if we were extending a dinner invitation to the wrong guest?

What if there were no other sentient beings out there to respond to our olive branches and greetings and salutations in eighty-eight tongues?

What if that power source was a natural pulsating phenomenon and not intelligently scripted?

NASA had to know one way or the other if only to appease Man's creationist supposition of being children born of three gods but one father.

The costs, although exorbitant, were never too high to induce vertigo. After all there was no price tag on Faustian[68] wisdom. That, too, was part of the deal with the devil we thought we knew from Sunday school.

The "momentum of anticipation," as the *Miami Herald Examiner* termed it, rallied us all around this giant maypole on Launch Pad 29 to dance and sing the praises of being alive at this very special moment in time. We all were smitten, even when we didn't understand the value of pi[69] that forever stutters in a cunning display of a broken record that no longer requires the services of a DJ.

What was even more absurd was the idea of something so great as Magellan 7 waiting for anything, much less three tiny men. To be both wondrous and intimidating was something only Science could conjure with its esoteric spells and mathematical witchcraft. How was it possible for something weighing over four-hundred thousand tons to not only get off the ground but to leave Earth's tugging atmosphere? To this day, it still staggers my mind. And in an ironic and final bizarre twist, three orphans were now to be the goodwill ambassadors for the family of man.

However, that was nothing to be outraged or ashamed about. Dick and Harry were in the top one percent of their graduating classes at NASA, making their promotions to Alpha Team a lateral step more so than a giant leap back. Every astronaut at Launch Level status had the proper stuffing and credentials so there were no radical drop-offs, regardless whose gravity boots had to be filled. But, as with all equals, there are some men who just can't be equaled.

Unlike the choice for Captain and Galactic Navigator aboard Magellan 7, there never was a festering doubt in regards its Science

Officer. No one could juggle equations quite like Tom Webster, the genius of Silicon Valley. Even the so-called experts at MIT and Cal Poly Tech found his expressions very insightful and revolutionary. His was a nimble mind that could process opposing brackets and expressions without once contaminating Celestial Mechanics[70] with Jiffy Lube grease monkeys. Of the newly formed trio, Tom was the group's vocal leader as well as senior member in frequent flyer miles logged. In fifteen years, Thomas Webster completed three missions to Mars, one to Jupiter, six to the lunar surface, and three to Space Lab 5.

But if Commander Webster was the smartest and most seasoned, then Dick was the handsomest, and Harry the more dour and reserved. All were prolific storytellers as all men with waxwings who volunteer to fly toward the sun. Their tales were said to be a mixture of two parts veracity and one part audacity. The mass media with its nightly liturgies ate it up and we digested it with each and every sound byte. Not even the most discriminating actuary could readily discern who was the youngest or oldest. All three men looked younger than their officially listed ages. Tom was 42, Dick, 39, and Harry, 37. Not only was their hair thick, full, and the blackest jet, but nowhere was it betrayed by a widow's peak or prodigal strand of gray. And their eyes! Their eyes were a Mendelian[71] cross between a royal and sky blue that were as deep as they were straightforward and determined.

These uncanny parallels never ceased to amaze a fawning, adoring public. Quite honestly, they looked more like favorite sons of the same milkman rather than spoiled nephews of a nepotistic uncle. These physical attributes and comparisons further fanned those vapors and wistful allegations that their coming together aboard Magellan 7 was meant to be; as if it was written in the stars before the beginning of recorded time and fast forward play. They really did seem too good to be true, yet there they were representing Old Glory, which also hadn't aged after all these many years.

Tom, Dick and Harry were everything national heroes were cranked up to be: smart, handsome, witty, and devilishly charming. Despite an over zealous security detail that hounded their every public appearance, they still were available for spontaneous autograph sessions, street interviews with ferreting reporters, and impromptu visits to local grade schools where their bigger than life personas inspired children to be better students in science, if only for the day.

It was a whirlwind romance, not only made in heaven but destined to return there. This puppy love affair was cause enough for keys to cities all across America. Our honeymoon with Tom, Dick and Harry showed no signs of slowing down or souring into contempt from over familiarity and a little too much information about fish and friends after three days. This feeding frenzy, as a matter of fact, only intensified as the launch date approached. It was incredible but we all had suddenly developed an insatiable sweet tooth for Tom, Dick and Harry.

I'd never seen anything like it. It was as if we couldn't get enough of those saccharine laced anecdotes that ran the gamut from what they liked to eat, to how it felt to float in zero gravity. We all just seemed to swirl as mad dervishes around their corner street pole of celebrity.

But as we stalked them, they in turn followed us in picture, print, and "oh by the way" anecdote. Sure, this schoolgirl crush was juvenile and intrusive but people didn't care whose toes they had to step on to get a better look at Tom, Dick and Harry. We just couldn't seem to get our fill of them in or out of uniform or off the official record when they could be men again and not simply heroes in orange and gold-fleeced jumpsuits.

The truly remarkable thing, however, was there was no shortage of tidbits. It never reached a saturation point or climax of enough being enough. Perhaps it was over compensation for a Nation's collective guilt. Who knows? Regardless the reason, we were in perfect pitched harmony with their iconic personifications of every other Tom, Dick and Harry. They became a living, movable piece of Americana that everyone wanted to see and touch before they embarked on their historic mission with our wagons in tow.

Yet strangely, it was only days earlier when nobody knew or even gave a damn why Harry joined the Thunderbirds or how Dick sustained that exotic cut on his roguish forehead. Their meteoric ascent to Alpha Team would have wilted lesser men. Dick and Harry, however, were unfazed by the limelight and sudden exposure as if they were aboard Magellan 7 from its genesis like Thomas Webster. Dedicated men on a mission are too obsessed to be distracted and led astray. Such is the fickleness of life, to languish in dungeons of obscurity, than bask, as a bathing beauty who just won a beauty contest that had no Apple of Discord[72].

There were so many firsts going on and about that it tempted narcissistic tendencies to explore other watering holes. It was also the first time three orphans were on the same mission. Sooner or later, conversations returned to this retention pond where you couldn't reflect upon anything else without first acknowledging that brazen, unbelievable fact.

I must admit it was a rather curious reversal of fortune, to be celebrating men, not for what they did, but for what they were about to do. Talk about putting the cart before the ass. Nevertheless, Tom, Dick and Harry were our favorite sons, if not by blood, than by an informal proxy that needed no handshakes to seal the deal.

In the court of public opinion, they were only guilty of being a little too perfect and precise with their P's and Q's. Needless to say, they had their own fan clubs, but by their own admission they were first and foremost a team with a single-minded purpose. Even their names had become synonymous with their long awaited calling to the stars between Ophiuchus[73] and Draco[74].

Tom, Dick and Harry made sure none were greater than the advertised whole.

This held steady and true whenever separated by prior personal engagements. It was remarkable how quickly they bonded and forged meaningful alliances of one for all and all for one common goal and mission. Although this flight crew sans Tom was NASA's second choice, it was now, without question, America's first preference whether waving hello, goodbye or just smiling for the ever present paparazzi forever jockeying for that one last money shot on the tarmac by Launch Pad 29.

CHAPTER FOUR

Seven Missing Links

WHEN I ARRIVED at Joe's house in West Palm a few days later, it was deserted. No cops, no agents, no evidence technicians. The emptiness only added to the lurid surroundings. The only thing different was an overdue library notice sticking out of the mailbox. That immediately struck me somewhat peculiar. I mean, why would a man who had a who's who list of expensive first editions in his private collection go slumming at the Miami Public Library? That was like marrying the Princess and drilling the chambermaid. It just didn't make any sense to dabble with midgets when you had literary giants at your fingertips. I knew Joe sometimes utilized unorthodox agencies during his search and destroy missions. Was perhaps this one of those times?

Joe, though, never divulged his sources until it was time to spring that Cheshire[75] from the bag. But only after establishing the lineage of pertinent facts that couldn't be refuted, disputed, or called into question in the old man's office upstairs. In that respect, Joe was as much a P.T. Barnum as he was a biographical auditor digging up dirt and petrified bones for an amused if not select audience.

I never knew Joe to go to the Public Library. It wasn't below him, it just wasn't in him.

There was nothing found at his house to create a hypothesis or for that matter apply it to some general theory relative to the investigation. As much as I tried, I couldn't build a biography on conjecture. Oh sure there was a timeline, but there was no working scenario to plug it into. And with no body of evidence to probe it was no different than trying to dissect a phantom.

The house, as a discrete suitor, surrendered nothing. It was unheard of for crime scenes of this magnitude to not be rife with calling cards. Pride and vanity tend to subconsciously leave behind genetic signatures. It went with the yellow taped territory. With the exception of Joe's blood and scattered fingerprints, however, the place was clean of clues to cobble together.

In most homicides, it's pay up or pay back. In Joe's case, this made no sense. But if it wasn't premeditated, it was a random act, which then precluded why someone would hack into his computer. I, however, couldn't accept Joe's murder being a random act of violence. White-hot crimes of passion by their very nature had a penchant for being sloppy with a cadre of leads to follow up on.

Nothing abounded to place anybody with Joe between last call at O'Brien's and eight o'clock in the morning when a Japanese gardener discovered his headless corpse gruesomely posed on the front porch. Lab rats[76] at Quantico said it was almost as if Joe up and killed himself, then dragged his lifeless body onto the alabaster portico. No signs of forced entry did lend some momentary credence to this aspect of the investigation. But as all unusual things, it too was soon relegated to that clueless slagheap just as that other ridiculous possibility that Joe was murdered by a ghost of many Christmas' past.

Spooks and invisible men were no more plausible than Joe allowing a complete stranger into his home, which was more an antique Emporium than a secluded mansion on the back nine at Palm Eagle Ridge. If one single thing jumped out, it was the utter chaos in Joe's house. The mansion wasn't just trashed, it was turned inside out. I'd never seen such a disjointed crime scene. Everything was tossed like a Caesar salad. Rookie cops executing search warrants for the first time never ransacked a joint like this. The liberties were that flagrant. The mischief from this microburst made me wonder if I wasn't onto another hellish descendent of Loki[77].

The laundry list of causes and becauses were extremely long. Was it burglary? Was it robbery? But Joe still had his wallet on him. He also had a forty thousand dollar diamond sprinkled Rolex strapped to his wrist. That more or less put the kibosh on robbery as a motive. Even the range of possibilities to the possibilities stretched beyond Ockham's Razor[78].

Was it an angry antique collector outbid on some ancient relic by Joe? That did satisfy a lot of criteria, primarily motive and opportunity. More precisely, it provided meaning as well as a coming to terms with this monstrous baby. It was also an angle the local rags[79] picked up and ran with after they discovered Joe frequented auction houses in Miami, Palm Springs, and South Beach. Antique collectors are generally not noted for being a violent lot, at least not outside bidding rooms where killings are symbolic. I must admit, though, it did give a much-needed boost to that numbers game of rotten apples existing in the same bushel as good ones.

Yet nothing was missing from Joe's multi-million dollar collection. The Monets, Rembrandts, Gauguins and Picassos were all in attendance. Everything of appraised value was studiously catalogued and accounted for throughout the mansion. That baffled me. Everything Joe owned was highly coveted, prized, and expensive. What's more, it easily could have been fenced on the black market in Miami. Anybody with half a brain surely would have known this eclectic collection was worth something, even if to somebody else. In the criminal parlance it would have made a good score much better. His Remingtons[80] for example, were valued in the three million dollar ballpark, a range most men would never see let alone squat upon. Yet sculpted masterpieces remained as if they were purchased at a Sun City[81] garage sale were junk as a general rule is found somewhere between a man's house and the garbage cans in the alley. And a killer so meticulous and cunning as this couldn't possibly be that naïve. It wasn't a personality fit, at least not in my makeshift profile.

Was it possible the killer was a man of principles? I could only hope not. Idealists not motivated by profit are the hardest to track because they leave no bread trails[82] to follow off the Interstate. Such psychopaths are generally loners, men who have no biological use for games that involve slap—and—tickle. In a perverse sense they're ascetics only their self-denial begins and ends with their pilgrimage to Homicide where their victims are sacrificed for no other apparent reason than being in the wrong place at the wrong time.

I always tried to get a visceral reaction from crime scenes before canvassing, processing, and triangulating any evidence. Joe's mansion, however, had so many inconsistencies that nothing could be taken for granted as a goodnight kiss at the front door. False roads, dead ends, and primrose paths seemed to be part of this butcher's specialty of three for the price of one.

Who was this mystery man? Was he a thrill killer?—A pattern killer?—Perhaps a spree killer? But what's the statistical probability of three people from NASA getting killed in three different places on the same night? Besides, adrenaline rushes didn't last that long for killers. You just don't kill a person here, a person there, and then hop in a car to go kill somebody else twenty-eight miles away. Their warped MO is more along the lines of rat—tat—tat. It's fast, furious, a flashpoint of muzzles indiscriminately spraying death as an exterminator void of conscience in regards Queen Mothers and working class drones.

On the other hand, revenge as a trigger was eternal as the Hatfield's and McCoy's. It has no time limits or physical boundaries. But like I said, Joe wasn't the type of man to provoke hatred in anyone, not even during games of cutthroat when friends were no more necessary than directions to a stubborn man lost in the middle of nowhere.

The specter of a green-eyed monster forever lurked concerning Joe's privileged pedigree. I could never factor jealousy out of any equation. Joe's entire family, however, was wealthy and well off. I'd known his two children, Jessie and Diane, since they were little kids. They adored Joe. He gave them everything they ever needed or wanted. What's not to like about a twenty-four seven Santa Claus on the premises?

I was obsessed with solving the why. In my experience why led directly to who. Another thing is, in over ninety percent of homicides the killer is known by his victim, which in Joe's case narrowed the field down to half of Martha's Vineyard. But rich people come from an over indulgent world of long greens, short putts, koi ponds, and discrete plastic surgeons who never put "33's on 78" [83]. Time could no more dictate to them than a ditzy secretary in a temp pool. As for myself, I couldn't imagine having a stock portfolio at birth. I learned long ago that buying silver spoons at Wal-Mart no more cut the mustard than it did a Gordian Knot [84]. Besides, socialites in those economic brackets are from very select and refined families who share the same hedge fund brokers and vintage bottlers of Dom Perignon, which begged the question, "why would a pampered stuffed shirt stoop to a level below their senatorial station and short list of things to do while in West Palm?"

Joe's college friends had just as much old money, so what would their motivation be? To have more of what they already had up the wazoo? Greed, however, was a very real thing that I couldn't discount or dismiss even amongst his Harvard frat brothers. Killing for the sake of killing also made no sense. It didn't even pay the bills. Yet those who enjoy the kill are far more lethal than those short fused crack heads that break down conventional wisdoms just to catch unconventional buzzes.

I scanned every possible depth chart of snowballs in hell, left-wing subversives, Nazi anarchists, Lizzie Bordenesque [85] family members with axes to grind, transients drifting through to the Keys on the lam from more than Old Man Winter. I couldn't completely rule out a domestic terrorist cell looking to tarnish America's image in her hour of glory and triumph. But why target Joe? Campbell and Snyder I could understand, but Joe was beyond the pail as misfits from the wrong side of the tracks exploding with powder keg syndrome.

I couldn't exclude a lone wolf predator feeding off his own psychopathic ego but that pointed directly to that affair with the mirror on the wall, a club exclusive to those young and restless at heart who wanted their "fifteen minutes" to last a lifetime.

It could very well be a young man; one even younger than the one assigned this faceless maniac by the FBI profiler. The fury and rage was befitting someone with a lot of pent up aggression.

Besides, who else could throw a big league temper tantrum and support it until it burned itself out? That was the sticking point, Young Turks didn't have enough goddamn sense to avoid detection, always salting clues and inwardly screaming for attention of "come get me copper."

Joe's house was one stage with many global affiliations and names, like Venus who is also known as Hesperus[86] and Lucifer[87]. This was one case where a closed coffin didn't say more about the killer than his victim. I may have been able to suspend disbelief but I couldn't argue with ignorance. I would have been better served discussing leniency with a lynch mob. For a time, I even resorted to reading blood patterns like some Roman augur[88]. Yet that rendered nothing to my ken[89] of knowledge. One thing I did know was that with each passing hour, leads were getting colder as November into December. It's only natural for trails to dry up. And guessing games at so early an impasse are a fool's quandary, no different than playing charades with a quadriplegic.

That's what made Joe's crime scene so unnerving—it was beyond explanation. Nothing could further scandalize the dead in hopes of shedding some newfound light through that opportunistic door where my foot was wedged. I should mention that even after follow-ups were conducted by the local authorities, there still were no leads or suspects to pin tails on.

In murder investigations, you first eliminate truth until all that remains are liars with alibis in various stages of undress. Oh sure, there were the usual derelicts and winos confessing to the murders but they were soon dismissed with a bologna sandwich back to their cardboard jungles.

Why, you ask, would someone take the blame for something they didn't do? To me, it was like taking medicine when you weren't sick. To take the heat for someone else was Christianity gone haywire. I could never accept self-sacrifice. It sounded too Middle Eastern, too 'where's my paradise vest with dynamite for Allah?' I guess I'm too westernized to understand martyr madness as a way to screw seventy-two virgins. Seventy-two whores perhaps, but seventy-two virgins? No way! Besides, when freedom is exchanged for three hots and a cot[90] it doesn't say much about the human condition, even as a last ditch effort to make holiday ends meet.

Everything at this preliminary juncture was crazy, just like three bloody crime scenes but only one vandalized house on Carthage Lane. Maybe a mad man was on the loose. But temporary insanity as a plea or reason was nothing more than grandstanding with that most paradoxical of theatrical alibis. Let's be serious, there are no curfews on sanity. If anything, it's a latent insanity that conceals the identity of Mr. Hyde from the respectable Dr. Jekyll.

But anything left open to the mutiny of interpretation is nebulous and vague. The same could be said about that fateful night when Joe called from O'Brien's Bar and Grill and said he had news, big news! What could be construed and implied from something so ambiguous?—Something big? For Christ's sake, getting a root canal was big. Such canvasses are much too broad and suggestive to paint a portrait of anything of substance that could be associated with any actual person of interest.

With Joe, however, every project he worked on was big. It's not to say he had a Napoleon complex or anything, it's just that his work at NASA was important to National Security and all that other patriotic mumbo jumbo of Nathan Hale, Paul Revere, and Sam Adams. In that homage, Joe was honest and forthright. He not only bought it hook, line and sinking of the Maine[91], he also sold it on a wholesale basis, and without once seeking partisan approval or fiscal compensation for being a spokesman for the "Gang of Fore[92]."

I always thought pictures were supposed to develop and materialize in the dark. In Joe's house the darkness only produced more negatives that would pass but never come to pass this way again. Wasn't that though the way of all things great and small, to hang around in the present until gift-wrapped for a tomorrow that never comes with the morning newspaper? I'd been to Joe's countless times over the years from birthdays to New Year's Eve parties, but never could I have foreseen this solitary visit. It's not that I couldn't believe it, it's just I didn't want to.

It sounds strange, but I felt Joe's presence in certain sections of the house. It was as if even in death he had a favorite chair and room to sit in. I knew I couldn't get sentimental and stuck in the mud on Memory Lane. I had to maintain focus and the promise I made to Jessie and Diane to track down this killer if it was the last thing I did. They were bold words for a one-eyed man who hadn't hunted a killer in twenty years. But in their inconsolable grief, and mine, I really didn't know what else to say.

What I saw and what I didn't want to see during my sight search still creates a dispute that blurs that tagline between real and make believe. When one thing began to show a glint of promise, it too soon faded to black as a grieving widow. Such is the hell of prospecting for leads in no man's land. But there are never any guarantees when plumbing depths beyond your league. That's the digging disclaimer upon every subterranean venture that seeks its treasures where the sun never shines.

Where to start was quickly becoming a recurrent theme that always brought me back to the Study, just like when I was a kid playing with Colonel Mustard, Miss Scarlet, and Professor Plum[93]. Only now it was for real, and not limited to the usual suspects or those oxidized wrenches, lead pipes, and smoking guns.

While dissecting crime scenes, one has to know where to cut one's losses and what to keep from "doughnut patrols[94]" that can't find their asses with both their sticky hands. That's how it is. Some things you publicly share, other things you keep secret with the four walls.

Blood and books were scattered everywhere throughout the study. It was said Joe was killed at his computer terminal, his lifeline to the world of yesterday. To be quite honest, I didn't know what I was looking for; half the time I didn't even know what the hell I was looking at. Joe's old things gave me the creeps. They made me feel like I was in a ghoulish nightmare with chalk outlines that told stories without authorship, footnotes, or happy endings.

Joe's books were the most displaced of anything in the mansion. Some were ravaged and torn asunder, leaving but a few measly shreds to cling to fractured spines. Every book was evicted from its numbered berth in first class. I should remind you that Joe's private library had well over two-hundred thousand books, with one classic tome more expensive than the next. It angered me to see Joe's labor of love reduced to this vile, barbarous display. Joe spent a lifetime, not to mention a small fortune, assembling this cast of characters. Of all Joe's worldly possessions, his books were his pride and joy.

I found this outward display of destruction by the killer, to be calculating and free of microscopic indictment yet foaming at the mouth. But that didn't make sense either. Clear-headed killers are never live wires. They have a cool to the touch persona of bullets without folksy ballads, of criminal thoughts abandoning emotions in mid-sentence of thirty years to life without parole. Maybe this act of vandalism was to destroy evidence or conceal clues? This malicious hooliganism was as unnecessary as it was unwarranted. The killer surely had to know this.—He had to. Someone so meticulous and thorough would not require a Plan B, or a 'just in case.'

Was a Luddite[95] directive wrapped in this enigmatic display? After butchering someone, that was like reading the fine print on a Gambino family[96] contract. Only in the study did any sort of tentativeness prevail. It was strange in a weird way; everything else was knocked over, yet every freestanding mahogany bookcase remained upright. It was almost as if they were being deliberately singled out and avoided by the killer. But if the killer was strong enough to carry Joe to the porch, he no doubt could have easily tipped over those wooden monoliths without a problem to his back or ego. This, as much as anything else, kept drawing me back to the Study.

Is this, perchance, where the killer blinked? Is this where he lost his nerve? Or is this simply where he regained his senses after going berserk? Maybe the vandalism was a smoke screen to conceal something far more insidious and sinister? Who knows, maybe the killer was looking for something the same way we frantically rifle through our belongings after misplacing something intimate and dear.

Every investigation is a series of structured procedures. In regards to sequence, of which way to pivot and turn, it was ponderous as an infinity sweep that scatters dust to every corner of the room. Where was that Theseusian[97] Thread in this maze of contradictions? I couldn't have felt any clumsier if I was a pickpocket wearing mittens. It is said that in order to catch a killer you have to first think like one. But how does one become a mad, deranged character with Walter

Mitty[98] scripts? Being cold blooded and pretending to have a heart of darkness are exact opposites albeit on the same magnet. Years ago, when I posed as someone else, it was to track down Minerva Keres, the Times Square Troller.

Four years is a long time to forsake your identity in pursuit of another's. Back then; all I had to work with was a hazy description of a raven-haired beauty with an ominous nickname, Kinky Baby. That's all I had when I descended into Hell's Kitchen to land that Man-eater working the sperm banks off Lower Manhattan's Viagra triangle. But never before have I had just one note, or in this case, library notice, to name that killer's tune.

In a way it's reassuring to know there are no empty beds in nut houses. Such is that Masonic rub[99], to have clean hands but a dirty mind that never gets out of the prophylactic gutter. Working on scraps of information from shoddy and choppy reports was not exactly conducive to determining what was and what wasn't distorted from one horse's mouth to the next, like several Biblical Jews who, with each successive passing, swelled into a multitude[100].

What was pertinent? Who was relative? Yet the longer I dwelt upon something, the more it tended to resonate to that bottomless pit where salvage operations were impossible to coordinate. Believe it or not, there are prick teasers for Revenge's hard-on too.

Nothing that day could be pinned down at the shoulders. Reasonable and unreasonable doubts infiltrated every case scenario. Absolutes, as you know, are hard to come by in any murder investigation, and that's when you have something credible to work with besides theories, long shots and wild hairs up your ass. Don't forget, there are no models of consistency when man stretches fact as fiction as a would-be[101] traveler in the next bed. Joe's study in a final twist had become the quintessential study in murder; only it had seven missing books and one subject to throw it at. If it were anyone else, I may have enjoyed the gallows humor. But like I said, I couldn't lower my guard. That's how I reinforced my own brand of McCarthyism[102], of seeing more than red wherever I looked. The things we do to maintain our perspective when fighting windmills[103].

Was Joe intentionally brought to the study, or did he instinctively come to his comfort zone, as men tend to do when fleeing something from their predatory past? The killer may have deviated here, but not Joe, never Joe. He was too fundamentally ordered to be steered off course or physically intimidated. Yet the County Coroner stated there were no gunshot wounds on Joe's body. That was another enigma because Joe was a big, powerful man who could easily handle most men half his age. That fact didn't mesh and color coordinate with his black belt in karate. His wounds were said to be a combination of defensive and post mortem. Some experts at the FBI claimed his wounds were the result of a torture ritual performed in medieval Europe. As for myself, I wanted to believe Joe went down fighting, but I secretly hoped his wounds were inflicted after death.

Everything became a monochromatic collage with a running commentary that could never be cut from that stampeding herd of 365[104]. Of course times, places, and names change but it's always man the constant dinner companion throughout thirty thousand years of Gorilla Theater. But who came first, the Abel-bodied victim or the fugitive East of Eden[105]? It rendered that chicken and egg conundrum somewhat hackneyed now as a farmers market in the middle of downtown Miami.

I knew there were myriad nightmares to analyze, but there was only one way to get to the Land of Nod[106]. What I discovered about myself that day was more than what I gathered at the crime scene. But don't all discoveries start with one, like all great counts that flee into Kasner's childish googolplex[107]? I told myself that I would run with whatever I found, however absurd, ridiculous, or insignificant, and take it to its logical conclusion. Who would've ever imagined my only viable lead, however, would be books? Not expensive, hard-to-find books, but public library books that anybody could finger and defile.

What interested me was not that they were taken out but why they were taken out in the first place. That was as elusive as those seven dwarfs' names. Despite public indecency having a generic cheapness, the sheer number of books scattered pell-mell in the Study made it virtually impossible to separate the borrowed from the bought. Besides, maybe the killer took those seven books. This was a possibility that was not without merit. I've known killers to take some rather unusual keepsakes and souvenirs from their victims. But who would mistake a public library book from Viking press for a treatise from an eighteenth century salon in Paris? Only a rube, that's who. And like I said, whoever killed Joe was no such creature of the shallows.

Was it possible the books had something to do with Joe's death? But library books and Joe didn't seem compatible, not even in the same sentence, let alone his last breath. If I had something more substantial to latch onto I might not have even given these seven missing links a flirtatious glance. Chance encounters, however, sometimes favor the ignorant that have been known to stumble upon mudders[108] even on sunny days at Hialeah.

CHAPTER FIVE

6 Faxes

I N THE WAKE of Joe's death, I was promoted team leader of the Bloodhounds. Not only did I inherit Joe's position, I inherited all the responsibilities of leadership up to and including end of pipeline clutter. I never saw an incoming box so pregnant with paperwork. Yet out of Joe's bloated chaos I was to somehow restore a semblance of order. The office was brimming with chimneys of work reports, time schedules, interview dates, personnel files, and other interagency memos and correspondences. Talk about a dark victory! No sooner than I had assumed musher status was I sifting through bureaucratic detritus[109]. It was one thing to separate files; it was another to make sense out of them. Joe may have died but that didn't stop this cancerous mass growing on his desk. Work, as life, must go on. After all, NASA was in show business too, only its stars were not limited to Broadway and Hollywood.

What caught my eye was a bold letterhead from the Illinois Public Guardians' Office in regards Richard Joseph Sanders and any and all available juvenile documents and photographs from 1981 to 1993 while at St. Michael's orphanage in Chicago. The request was just as strange as Joe's sudden interest in Dick Sanders' childhood. It had been nearly ten years since Joe and I concluded our interviews with Dick Sanders. If any follow-ups occurred they were initiated a few days after the final pre-candidate screening process when you still had doubts and reservations about the validity of a particular space cadet. But never did we dig into a candidate's childhood. If candidates were padding or tuck—pointing holes in their story it was always during their adult years.

What was so urgent and important about an orphanage Dick Sanders stayed at while growing up in Chicago, one that had been reduced to cinder twenty-seven years before with great loss of life? Under the cover sheet was a manila envelope with Department of Children's Services memos and photographs of St. Michael's.

Graphic stills of a charred and gutted building along with six faxes of government blather were all that remained to prove the orphanage once existed in time and inner city space. In and by themselves the photographs were not all that unusual. After all, buildings burn down every day. With respect to St. Michael's, no consensus ever put to rest the true cause of the blaze. After years of squabbling on whether it was an accident, an act of God, or arson, the Illinois Fire Commission concluded the firestorm was caused by spontaneous combustion that originated in grease traps located directly below an improperly vented boiler room.

Even to those old enough to remember this modern day Iroquios Inferno[110], as it was called in the *Chicago Tribune*, it was all but cemented over and deleted from public consciousness. That is until Dick Sanders was thrust into the national spotlight. Before his ascension to Alpha Team nobody but Joe gave a rat's ass about a torched home for indigent orphans on the Southside of Chicago. Up until then, it was nothing more than stenographic endnotes to a court long since adjourned from alternative explanations and malingering conspiracy theories.

Due to shoddy workmanship, the conflagration raced uncontested throughout St. Michael's. Children and adults were instantly vaporized. Anything in its incendiary path was mercilessly consumed. Classrooms, record departments, dorms, halls, even the administrative offices were totally destroyed. Outside the suspicious origins of the fire nothing appeared out of sorts. You might say it was all by the numbers, from the initial call to the 911 Center at

8:35 a.m. to the 6-alarm fire that claimed the lives of 236 children and 28 Catholic Charities staff members on August 8, 1993.

Did Joe perhaps have some additional information concerning the fire at St. Michael's? Or was he just ahead of the bandwagon and curve in regards Dick Sanders? Did Joe think Dick Sanders had something to do with that deadly fire twenty-seven years ago? Dick Sanders, however, was only twelve years old at the time. It's not to say he couldn't have started the fire. I knew all too well that Mystery and Abomination[111] has no age requirements.

I tried to look beyond the squares of red and black[112] that had public coronations for kings. What you sometimes don't see is far more important than what you might want to. After all, the power of observation is also an art form, only its nudes were not always on draped pedestals but stainless steel slabs at the County Morgue.

Perhaps Joe was interested in why Dick Sanders was the lone survivor from St. Michael's? Joe failed to recognize dumb luck as an intangible concerning the thinning of the herd. Was it any wonder he openly dismissed the 1969 Mets? Any game that offered fools an equal opportunity at the brass ring defied Joe's principal line of reasoning, of the strong surviving to fight another Lost Cause. But as any discipline found amongst Delphic ruins[113] and alligator wood[114], a man was to trust his instincts. And Joe, as leader of the Bloodhounds, had that repossessor's knack for looking under rocks when others were content to play ducks and drakes[115].

After the summary on the blaze concluded, the report shifted its focus to the young Dick Sanders. "Per your request, no juvenile photos exist in Illinois State file for Richard J. Sanders," a curious snippet leapt off the page, nabbing my attention like a kick to the groin.

It was hard to believe not one single picture existed of young Dick Sanders. It was almost as if his entire youth had been physically erased. If a fire's one thing, it's an equal opportunity destroyer. But there were probably hundreds of orphans who didn't have photos of themselves while growing up on the State's dime. What's the sense of capturing a white elephant[116] for posterity? Besides, who wants to revisit Hell in black-and-white or color? It could be argued that the reason nothing survived Dick Sanders' youth was because nothing was worth saving in the first place.

Sure it was unusual, but it wasn't unheard of to not have a photograph to tell a thousand words let alone one endearing appellation[117]. Some kids, by their very nature, are camera shy and embarrassed about their awkward, gangly affiliations. Other kids, to round out the seating arrangement, don't even attend their own school proms or get their driver's license until they are free of acne, braces, and seventh period gym.

Prior to basic training at Lakeland Air Force Base in 2004, Dick Sanders was nothing more than a faceless entity passing through life's prickly turnstiles. Though there might not be old photos of him on file, there most certainly had to be a self-portrait hidden in some garret asylum[118]. I mean, the guy hadn't aged a day from his enlistment photo. You'd swear that high and tight[119] was cropped yesterday and not sixteen years before. Nothing betrayed or sabotaged his moratorium on youth. Maybe it was his diet? Maybe it was exercise? Maybe it was good genes? Whatever the hell it was would have envied Dorian Gray at a Botox party in Beverly Hills.

What was Joe interested in finding out? Trying to get into a dead man's head was harder than getting into a sober woman's pants. It was akin to pulling hen's teeth with a GED in dentistry. If Joe wasn't willing to tip his hand, you were doomed to relive Pearl Harbor. Of any man I've ever known, and I've known CIA spies, Joe was the only one who could isolate his thoughts to the point of quarantine.

Still the question remained: why? It made no sense. For one thing, NASA did not require photographs of candidates when they were juveniles. In twenty years I never once initiated a juvenile photo search, and neither did Joe, until Dick Sanders.

If Dick Sanders wasn't female eye candy, I could understand his ugly ducking bashfulness and dread of the lens for this photographic void. But this Adonis[120] was a natural for the limelight. Surely someone so handsome just didn't get that way overnight. Needless to say, a camera can lie, but not his, never his. Low self-esteem might be many things but blind is not one of them. It just didn't make sense, for even as children we want to be remembered for something other than a number in a cafeteria conga line. But does social engineering ever fully get around to that gap in our arrested development? Or is it only one more stage stuck in neutral between furry cocoons and a monarch's maiden flight to Mexico?

With every dance there's a key. This dance with the dead was no different. But what was the numbered sequence to this tarantella[121] madness? One's point of view, after all, depends on where you stand on the death penalty and where you kneel come Sunday morning. In that respect, I suppose rainbows are similar to federal pens with their vertical bars and distinct holding patterns that mutate from cell to cell as raindrops that become solids, liquids, and gasses.

I flitted across the report with its sketchy lineage of runaway slaves from chain stores. Not only were there holes in Dick Sanders' physical record, there were also skips on his school record too. In and by themselves these juvenile gaps weren't that detrimental. When lumped together, however, they created some rather interesting breaks that couldn't be bridged by friendly acknowledgment or government statistic. How was it possible that nothing could be verified, documented, or substantiated? I know frames of reference aren't perfect but this bordered the unbelievable even for bureaucratic blunders.

Skipping school was one thing; skipping town after St. Michael's burned down was a whole other name dropping game, one the young Dick Sanders seemed to excel at. Like a mushroom, he grew in the dark, prospering as a looter during a rolling blackout. But even without documentation, there was no sugar coating his young life as a runaway. Naked truth can never be clothed or warmed by Bohemian fires in parking lots, homeless shelters, or bus terminals.

I suppose losing anything, including one's childhood, was painful enough. Maybe it's just the underlying concept of the whole goddamn thing, you know, of a loss being a loss whether a Massachusetts Mandarin[122] or street urchin[123] of Fagan[124]. We all have trouble dealing with things on the other side of the dirt ledger. Still, we don't run away and bury our heads in the sand for years at a time. But regardless if you drank yourself under the table or not, what was important was knowing what to keep sacred and who was to be forsaken after your fly was zipped up.

I darted across pages running from one indictment and sentence to the next. I couldn't help but recall the first man to run a marathon also collapsed at the finish line. Was that a forewarning or fitting tribute to all men in wingtips and Nikes?

The years become their own wax curse. But ignoring or lying about the number of candles on your cake will never erode that Rock of Ages. Not even salty tears will do the trick. It never changes either. It plays the same song every day, month, and year for everyone regardless if you believe in Jesus, Vishnu, Mohammed, or Yahweh.

With destiny there are no accidents, no wrong turns on fire escapes. A man can no more damn torpedoes than circling hungry hammerheads. But did one have to know the sender to get the gist of that message in a bottle? Premeditation, unlike spur of the moment, has surprise on its dark side just as anarchists[125] who alone know when death is to be meted out in the marketplace. Triggers, as latent hostilities, are undetectable until they creep into weekend police blotters. Those inner workings remain imperceptible as gears of a Swiss cuckoo, which although considered crazy, still have a rabid contingent of followers to sing its quarterly praises[126].

I jumped from one hotline to the next. Sure we might journey on separate back roads in search of truth and justice, but in the end we all meet in the same viewing room. It was as if Joe went in pursuit of sadistic sirens[127] that were more into wrecks than toothless hillbillies at the Indy 500.

It was a clean sweep of a dozen years that had no moral high ground to suffer or condemn. Nothing was known of Dick Sanders' mother, father, or next-of-kin. Even his foster parents were deceased. But everything was like that; it was unfounded, unknown, dead, or not located in the Illinois Database.

I knew Joe prided himself on being a bio-analyst, but was this background search of Dick Sanders going a little too far? Still I couldn't help but wonder what he was looking for. After all, ambition only gives the impression of not having a hidden agenda. That's the cultural epitome of office politics: to have two faces but only one five o'clock shadow.

But of anything, facts were Joe's drug of choice. He derived truth serum not from natural decay, but a man made analytical obsession. When it came to tracking a man's whole story, Joe was a relentless bounty hunter.

I snorted more and more lines, getting more and more addicted to this down and dirty that had long ago matured in the human psyche. However, getting the bureaucratic shuffle tended to provoke subversive feedback, like hot cookies and kleptos with cold glasses of milk. But even if there were no hell to pay, man surely would have invented that bill of fare. The Public Guardian related everything there was to know about nothing. At this time, at that time, at present time, in regards the young Dick Sanders, it was all the same goddamn time.

People forget innocence exists only once without a suitcase. How can children rationalize random acts when the Universe is supposedly a well-oiled machine created by intelligent design? Yet it's by that same said reasoning that drive by shootings corroborate and make the Big Bang complete.

I grabbed and gobbled the sixth and final page when Dick Sanders suddenly vanished from the statistical radar screen. For eleven years, he would be missing in action as a flophouse vagabond until July 2004 when the self-taught wunderkind emerged in the United States Air Force as Airman R. J. Sanders. From that seminal date forward nothing in Dick Sanders' life was divorced from the norm. Every event, every school, every test, every qualification was officially noted and properly documented. Only two men, Thomas Webster and Henry Collins, went through the ranks faster than Dick Sanders. His rise notwithstanding was still meteoric. He was first in his graduation class at flight school, war ace with forty confirmed kills, elite pilot for the Thunderbirds, top gun prodigy, first in his class at Navigator school. On and on accolades and awards were given him. It was said with no exaggeration that he had more ribbons and medals than a Bolivian dictator. I believe it. After all, I did review his service record that was as outstanding as it was impeccable. After reading his service record I really didn't need to play any other permanent record. You might say it closed the deal for me. It was easy enough to do. Who wouldn't be blinded by all those bright and shiny medals on his proud chest? Besides, I could relate to having no parents while growing up, which I believe is why I had an affinity for Dick Sanders and his cocky edge that was confident without being arrogant.

What made this Requisition Order even more unusual was the paperwork was submitted the same day Joe checked out those seven books from the Miami Public Library.—Coincidence?—Connection? I didn't know what to make of it. When one thing cleared the trees, another entered the forest canopy. Maybe Joe didn't buy that Fire Commission story? After all, something so awful and tragic doesn't ordinarily manifest itself without some sort of assistance from man. Who, though, couldn't assume the worst, not only in man, but about him?

What other angle could Joe be playing and why with the young Dick Sanders? How could an astronaut so famous, handsome, and smart be bad for anything, including a Nation's image? That also made no sense on any company level.

No sooner did I finish the report on Dick Sanders than I was on my way to the Miami Public Library.

CHAPTER SIX

Five More Cattons

AT THE LIBRARY, I was supplied not with a list of seven books, but twelve, only these five Catton's had been returned without so much a notice or nickel changing hands. It was the damnedest thing for the list of books the Head Librarian supplied me with were all on the American Civil War. It was redundancy being redundant.

How could this possibly be? It was so out of character for Joe. For one thing he wasn't a collector, and that invariably set the tone as well as the price for everything else to follow. He wasn't what you'd call a casual buff either. As a matter of fact, Joe didn't even have a Civil War book in his literary harem until a month before he was murdered. I remember when he called from Christie's in New York with the news of his purchase of an original photo journal by Matthew Brady for seventy-seven thousand dollars. He was so excited to have finally obtained the first master of photographic canvas, the man who "froze death for posterity and The Atlantic Monthly." I don't think I had ever heard Joe more satisfied or pleased. I suppose it's like anything else. Some see beautiful wedding videos while others see elaborate snuff films[128] with accelerated death benefits.

Was Matthew Brady perhaps the catalyst in whetting Joe's appetite for all things Civil War?—But twelve books, and all at the same time? I couldn't help but hoist a red ensign on the Flagship Suspicion.

Why the sudden fanatical bent? Joe never went overboard like this before. Was it possible it was the all-consuming first phase of a recently indoctrinated neophyte? Maybe Joe was just in a hurry to compensate for lost time? Maybe it was just his angst in regards to a literary shortcoming? The seven missing books were just like the five Joe brought back to the library the day before he was killed; all were written by the Civil War historian Bruce Catton and nuggeted with corresponding daguerrotypes[129] by Matthew Brady. Oh sure, the search may have been whittled down, but it was still like looking at the moon through the wrong end of a telescope.

Could Joe have been taking notes for a project? Or did he simply develop an insatiable jones for the Civil War as told by Catton and seen by Brady? I was hard pressed as a penny pincher at a wishing well. Still, knowing when to say something was tantamount to knowing when to say it with conviction. But was it possible for Joe to absorb twelve books, twelve thick books, on his hectic schedule?

Joe wasn't a speed-reader anymore than an impromptu one. I also knew he never wasted time dabbling in things that had no consequence or bearing to something else. Joe was not whimsical. He even detested the frivolous word 'hobby.' That's just how he was. Everyone and everything was in its proper time and place. Some people meddle without regard to Time's passage. Joe, on the other hand, measured life in seconds that could be split like a mama's boy's lip.

There were many contradictions in this Greek Chorus. It could be a dozen possibilities or a dozen more pieces of the puzzle. I hated that old math, you know, of taking something away only to leave behind a survivor of another's number crunch.

It could very well be a research project. After all, Joe did say he wanted to write a composite book on early manned flight in America. Flying was one of Joe's more demonstrative activities. And if anybody could write a book on flying, it was Joe. It was the primary reason he gravitated to NASA.

Beyond marbled swaths of observation balloons, however, there was little else to warrant such an extensive search. Some books never even acknowledged this lighter than air phenomena. When this pregnant creation with strings attached was alluded to, it was primarily topical in its homage and heavenly dedication, skimming the surface with only a few salted particulars of that Agency with the Angels. Surely there were other more in depth, comprehensive books on early manned flight to study and research. And Joe, more than anybody, would have known this.

Nothing was exactly revealing, not even on those select pages accented by his cryptic shorthand. Many were the names, faces and dates bandied about in endless paragraphs and seeded photographs. But as in all high profile endeavors, most men are bit players more so than any actual threat to one man's eventual claim to fame.

Despite marginal annotations in bubbly sections, Joe's mindset at the borrowed time was still completely unknown. And all ignorance does is grant license to wild goose chases and private refrains of glory hallelujah.

Unlike Joe, I preferred the company of contemporary things, things that had a pulse beyond past participles and auction houses. I was the Here and Now to his Gone and Forgotten. That's what made us the best one-two tandem in the sixty-three year history of the Bloodhounds. To me, everything prior to today was mawkish and antiquated to the point where it could no more fill shoes of clowns than fishermen. I don't know, maybe it's just the fact that it's old and over the fucking hill. I know it's all in a name, like used and pre-owned. But seriously, if that French aberration were called a Puerto Rican poodle how many rich assholes would still want to own one, let alone own up to having one?

I couldn't make a connection, not only to then and now, but also to Joe and Civil War books. It was crazy but no more crazy than putting your trust in library books during the Computer Age. Such anachronisms made emotional wrecks seem more salvageable. I remained at the Library until closing time, and then proceeded with the twelve books back to my house in Pompano. I have to admit; once I started sniffing I couldn't stop. It was as if the momentum from the word before pushed me across those lines of blue and gray. But I knew deep down inside I was onto something.—But what?—Scorched earth on Yankee turf?—What?

What significance could these books possibly have after all these years? Joe's mindset was paramount; if I only knew what he was thinking about at the time. Sure it was a stretch, but what else did I have besides a juvenile report, a burned down orphanage, and a dozen books on the Civil War?

I read and read and read some more. Still, after that first night, I could only add dry throat, bloodshot eye, and stiff neck to the witch's cauldron. As the scorned say, "there are no runaway trains, only cold feet at the altar."

I was pissed. Who wouldn't be? To do anything for so long without results is aggravating, and this search in futility was no different. Can any of us be exonerated from patricide, of killing Father Time? Yet in spite of these frustrations and setbacks, nothing else mattered to me. Everything now, including sleep and NASA, was secondary to these Civil War books, that as I consumed them they consumed me.

Confusion, which led down the Rapidan[130] to the Wilderness[131], also bled to postage stamps of real estate in the Gettysburg Address area code. Lines of attack and Hooker[132] descent symptomatically followed bloody trails littered with grapeshot[133], rebel yells and amputated limbs that never fell far from the family tree. Virginia, Pennsylvania, Georgia, Tennessee and Alabama weren't changes of venue, but only more places to die a thousand deaths before nightfall. Destroying Angels[134] were not only outfitted in white flesh but brazen uniforms that were not always blue and gray. Even volunteers were far greater than the ephemeral[135] roles they were assigned and ill equipped to play.

Rigor mortis glacially locked poses in developed place, preserving trained dummies for showroom windows of Eternity. Death had no favorites, no age requirements. It was the same everywhere, from Bloody Kansas[136] to Manassas[137] and every state of insanity in between. Did man intentionally precipitate war to elevate his status from private citizen to Brevet[138] General? Peace makes babies, but war makes heroes and matinee idols. We read Homer not for the poetry, but for the warriors who fought for a much greater union beyond Abraham.

Nothing appeared as it seemed with the rank or defiled. Southern man could no more escape his tyrannical calling than a fettered thrall[139] on a Richmond auction block. Advance, withdraw, and attack. The cycle was as vicious as it was never ending. Names and reputations were molded and transformed into one as Stonewall[140], Swamp Fox[141], and Bloodiest Man in American history[142].

Both sides perished with equal notification wherever grapes of wrath were crushed by bare foot or combat boot. Battlefields were christened by the nearest host town or body of water, the North invoking one nom de guerre[143] while the South nominated another to represent their stars, bars and racial stereotypes. The North and South couldn't even agree on the same name for the same blood orgy.

Still I had a yawning sensation that something was slanted, even when everything was right there in front of me, six feet in the perpendicular. Nothing, however, was administered on a small scale. This sanguine canvas was obsessed with hundreds of battlefields and millions of men. Although there were exhaustive maps, there were no trial canaries to send down into Stygian[144] shafts where those darkest secrets of man dwelt.

The unknown gives as much doubt as stories told by super liars[145] to wizards[146]. Still the question remains: how bad do you want to know in order to get better? In the final analysis, that's what determines how far any of us are willing to go. Going the extra yard is nothing; it's going those other ninety-nine that make all the difference in the world.

My red eye flight had its needle stuck on North and South as if they were the last two destinations and headings in the World. Not possessing the original seven books was a handicap due to their replacements being indicted by an entirely different agenda. In five Cattons I could easily follow Joe's left-handed script. Twenty years of office memos and Hallmark greeting cards made me somewhat of an expert in regards to Joe's ridges, loops, and slanted squiggles.

But which marks were coded and relevant and which were sleep commas and piss breaks? Deciphering shorthand is difficult enough, and that's when it's not self-styled and in conjunction to something mysterious and unknown. I tracked initials, abbreviations, acronyms, and numerical and alphabetical combinations and sequences. Mostly I was looking for a flow from chapter to chapter and book to book. What made my task more difficult was Joe had a savant's[147] knack for enlisting fighting words when no other apparent meaning was available beyond referenced milestone.

In five books Joe's prints were still warm and fresh, and although not anything to build shrines upon they nonetheless bridged gaps with their initial trajectory. But was US for General Grant?—Uncle Sam?—The United States? Or was it just us, as in you and me?

Needless to say, speculations ran roughshod over many signs and symbols. And without governors to regulate the flow between Bull Run[148] and bullshit, it was sometimes impossible to know where to portage and pick up Joe's stream of consciousness. But I knew the truth wasn't missing, even if its references were.

Still, what did *4th rock, P. L., Int.,P/C, d/l f/m, pic.by M.B. on 234* mean?

Pitched battles sold nothing but more death. Not only was time shot without a last cigarette, but it wasn't allowed to speak any final parting words. True to form, Time stood still even when running concurrent to that other sentence of march or die. Was I through a concoction of desperation and revenge reading too much into these Civil War tea leaves? I could never quite overlook that possibility, regardless of how blind I became.

Even in the most celebrated of Causes, man needs something more to fill his heart besides piss and vinegar. It doesn't necessarily have to sound sweet or taste good; all it has to do is hit those G-spots beyond proclamations and emancipations.

Drafts and winds of war became a formality as blue bags, recyclable compounds, and skeletons of Andersonville[149]. The parallels to slaying anything on four legs were consistent with man's evolving appetite in motels, studios, and battlefields. Green pages turned to a much older vintage, bringing forth the pale horses of plague, famine, destruction, and Robert E. Lee. Death came slow or very fast where a man was pronounced dead before he hit the consecrated ground.

Knowing the victims of war is never essential to solving crimes against humanity. Like most damnable offenses, it didn't require a coin toss to determine first stringers from benchwarmers with splinters in their asses. It also reconfirmed the natural order of things, that someone had to kick ass and someone had to receive a beating. Such is the epic "came, saw, conquered[150]" battle of life.

At times, it was a divine comedy with buffoonish clowns trying to maintain trade balances between calcified casts and train schedules. It's not that brothers were killing brothers but rather strangers were killing strangers in strange lands over a very peculiar institution[151].

I continued tracking as night followed day and day again trailed night. Hump day[152] turned to Thor's retreat[153] and anvil poundings echoing inside my war weary head spiked with chocolate, nicotine and triple shot café noir[154]. After two days I had to inquire, was I onto something or was I just chasing a tail of a shaggy dog that dizzies itself in pursuit of something it can only hope to catch after playing dead?

I hadn't done anything this irrational since arriving at NASA to the parroted taunts of "welcome aboard matey." But isn't level headedness the prelude to that retro caricature of the crew cut age when boys constantly need approval and a friendly pat on the ass after crossing home plate with the winning run? And to me, being practical with this strange and unusual case was really no different than playing Russian roulette with an automatic pistol.

CHAPTER SEVEN

4th Balloon Regiment

O F ALL THE words, numbers, and parenthetical manifestations, the *4th-Rock* was by far the most ubiquitous being scattered across five books and nearly six-thousand pages. But as with most formulaic abbreviations, it was ambiguous, like lead that is known as Pb on the Periodic Table. Was it perhaps an allusion to Mars? Or the mythological God of War? Or did it have something to do with horoscopes? But Joe believed in Jesus. And there was no ad-libbing in that script even when a beat was skipped between Lucy[155] and modern man.

Guesses beget more guesses as ignorant project bunnies that couldn't correlate a booty call with a baby born nine months later. I scoured pages, but I could no more change the outcome of Pickett's Charge[156] than caution a plodding thespian trapped inside an idiot box[157].

Other abridged abatements were in some instances just as conspicuous as the *4thRock*. But even after back tracking and cracking Joe's unique shorthand code, what did the 4th Balloon Regiment, rockoons[158], Professor Thaddeus Lowe, the spy balloon Intrepid, the Peninsula Campaign, downloading "fish matches", and a photograph by Matthew Brady on Page 234 have to do with anything?

My search seemed better suited for a skip tracer rather than a caffeine-laced hobbyhorse. Time and time again I was brought back to flight, and although this full circle explained some things, it didn't explain everything. What did Joe want to download; and what about those rockoons of the 4th Balloon Regiment? I had never seen or heard the word rockoon before. Not many did, other than the most erudite Civil War scholars who chronicled those primitive rockets launched from observation balloons.

During war, there is no distinction between life and death. One bleeds into the other as a hemophiliac from an incestuous line of royal inbreeds with big ears and short memories. There is no escape from that bloody chain of events, for they not only bind us as brothers in arms, they also hold us in contempt for an oxymoronic sight unseen.

How is it possible to be farsighted but unaware of things right underneath our noses?

Conventional wisdom, much like the twelve books, was soon exhausted in their use to me. To think, more Americans were killed during the Civil War than in all other conflicts combined. It says a lot about our mob mentality, you know, of taking care of our own. Beyond that, they didn't yield much else other than the fact there was no photograph by Matthew Brady on page 234 in any of the library books. But if the twelve books didn't garner anything of substance, what would that book by Matthew Brady in Joe's private library bring to my stable of errand boys?

Was turning over a new leaf just more semantics, like night owls and insomniacs? It's strange in a way, but I knew I'd be returning to Joe's house. Call it a hunch, a premonition, or a lucky guess. Call it what you will, but I knew I'd be going back, if not as a returning conqueror, then as one who didn't have anything else to smell, bark at, or chase up a tree. Such was my Catch-22, to return to Ground Zero on a flight of fancy.

One more book. It now sounds so innocent and trite, like the player to be named later who litters the waiver wire at the end of the baseball season. Frankly, after twelve books I was really in no mood to press my luck with thirteen. Don't forget, by that third day I was a zombie running on the exhaust fumes of midnight oil. Even my bed had become a distant memory. But that's how it is when you keep expecting a break in the case at any minute.

That afternoon, Joe's house seemed further away than ever before. Maybe the finality of it all was just starting to seep in, you know, of the last leg being the longest to "Old Sparky[159]." Commutes, as all fights in time and space, are a series of lefts and rights. But the concrete gained is neither sacred nor valuable as all bloodless revolutions on highways.

With the exception of tattered yellow streamers stubbornly clinging to fluted colonnades, the mansion seemed open to suggestion and familiar footsteps in the foyer. However, the mansion hid a secret as the shiny apple a worm. Yet not all queries warrant answers or even scholarly debate. It was as Lady Luck who could be pinched but not counted on in a pinch. But as sitting ducks had to be trained to sing like stool pigeons, so did crime scenes.

The past didn't resemble the present anymore. It was a separate entity altogether, like tiny acorns that, regardless of squirrels with good memories, still become mighty oaks. Knocking on wood or ringing bells was no longer a prerequisite for entry into the mansion. Those despotic habits couldn't be severed and spliced together with electrical tape. My doggish proclivities cursed this agent of radical change, to go from host to family and friends to maggots and grubs overnight.

Since my last visit, others had been here, if not to take something for a memento moiré[160] then to put a semblance of order back into the place. Walls were washed and painted, floors polished, pedestals reset. Bookcases were again restocked with fallen giants who had again tasted dust. Although books were back where they belonged vertically, they were devoid of Dewey[161] and out of whack alphabetically.

A stale odor of death still milled throughout the Study. The musty stench seemed to take on a hermetic life of its own. Yet oddly it couldn't be traced or attributed to any one particular source. And ironically, the scent was as exclusive as it was commonplace.

With so many books, over a quarter million, where does one begin? The endeavor made looking for a flea between the pillars of Calpe[162] and Jebel Musa[163] a more favorable prospect. I never realized the scope and breadth of Joe's authored tentacles. I recalled the book being black and not very thick, maybe two, three inches at most.

Despite not being anorexic, it still could be bullied by those giants and titans living posthumously in this airtight cave. Beyond black parchment and fashionably waifish, however, there was nothing else save the book's title to narrow and pare the field.

Black and white that sits side by side at kitchen tables, but rarely at them, was just one of the many imposing hedgerows in this laddered labyrinth[164]. Up and down, back and forth. The search for four years of spilling red to free black from white was protracted as an amputee waiting for the other shoe to drop.

Identification in this morgue became a ghoulish procession of fingering the dead whose thoughts lived on as another form of energy that never dissipates. But looking for a leather-jacketed punk at a black-tie affair was like trying to understand calculus as something other than a stony deposit that accumulates on the teeth. Then it hit; "Bull Run to Appomattox," a Civil War pictorial by Matthew Brady.

I extracted the black tooth ever so gingerly; afraid its brittle spine might snap. I had never held something so old or expensive before. And, notwithstanding its lineage, the photographs showed remarkable contrast and clarity. I immediately recognized some of the photos from the library books. However, the majority were as fresh to me as they were that day when they were first introduced to a shocked and outraged public. Photos brought the war home again, only this time for its latest captive audience. History as you know has a way of re-opening old wounds.

The written word was now strictly complimentary, with literary doses at pictorial intervals to set the stage for a particular day or specific battle. Canton utilized photographs as visual aides de camp[165], whereas Brady employed threadbare literary devices, allowing his camera to more or less speak for itself. But regardless if there was one line or five lines prefacing a photo, it was overkill all the same.

Page upon page capsulated man's fight or flight paradox. The aftermath of battle when body counts were taken was the majority stockholders in this smug enterprise of read'em and weep.

By a morbid twist, the lens, as the barrel of a gun, was indiscriminate in taking soldiers down Eternity Row. This grave chill pervaded all trenches and cold harbors[166]. Despite the fact that there were hundreds of pictures, it was still the same story developed time and time again.

After my melancholic curiosity waned, I proceeded to Page 234. To my surprise, the photo was sheared from the black and white herd. Beyond being hurriedly wrenched from the book, no other clinical details were available to name names or identify the kidnapped. All that remained was a bold heading at the top of the page that read, "Peninsula campaign, March 17, 1862".

Crude, jagged edges were neither time worn or acidically discolored, indicating the photograph was very recently removed from the book. Why would Joe intentionally disfigure his pride and joy? You just don't embezzle a photo from your own gallery. Such contradictions weren't in Joe's character any more than his spacious vocabulary. Besides, I knew for a fact that Joe purchased this book in mint condition. That was another of his pet peeves that celebrated totality and oneness.

What was so special about this particular photo that it had to be violently ripped out of a very expensive book? That was as perplexing as the word "SCAR" hurriedly scrawled by Joe in the adjacent margin.

The more possibilities swelled, the more the strike zone expanded. But if it wasn't Joe who confiscated this photo, then who did?—And why? Was it the killer perhaps? But why would the killer take one photo when he could've taken the whole goddamn book? That made no sense either.

Page 234 was the only page with a photo missing. The remaining pages in this ghastly gallery were not violated by theft or carbon apostile[167]. What was so special about this photo from the Peninsula campaign? That kept harping on me. I knew what I had to do and where I had to go. To tell you the truth, I'd rather watch paint dry than return to that death trap of yesterday where four-eyed monitors[168] prowled for waywards to chew out and eat alive as disobedient children of Saturn[169].

To me, a library was nothing more than a mausoleum where the dead communicated to the living. It was a place where holding your tongue was not just a test of endurance, but of one's resolve to abide by a draconian[170] rule that insisted silence was golden even when taken to those Nietzschean extremes[171] of "black dresses and silent parts". But isn't that part of our static proliferation to pass through time without being called a necrophiliac who prefers the company of the dead?

What other reservoir was available to tap? The possibility of the public library downtown having a copy of this photo album by Matthew Brady wasn't even a rumor to contemplate. What it did have, however, were schools of microfiche, and where else would Joe have 'gone fishing'?

CHAPTER EIGHT

3 Schools of Fish

I DIDN'T KNOW WHAT I was actually looking for, other than a photograph dated March 17, 1862. Still I had to wonder how wide the swath was going to be. Matthew Brady was quite the shutterbug. However, he was not alone in this mercuric spectacle of delivering death to the home front. He was only the most famous of the original horror masters of film. Did this particular photo make the transition to newspaper or some other publicly oriented medium? After all, that was the only way it would be preserved for posterity, unless of course the photograph was so famous that it didn't require public agencies to keep its appearance up. Maybe it stood by itself for something other than Harper's Ferry and John Brown's body? It very well might be famous in its own copyright.

My anxieties were somewhat dispelled by an assistant curator at the library who informed me another man had just recently requested these same three spools of microfiche covering the years 1861 to 1863. I knew I was following in somebody's footsteps, but were they Joe's? The scholarly matron couldn't recall anything specific about the previous user other than the fact he was tall, "like a basketball player."

Isn't it remarkable how quickly intimates are forgotten? But don't you find it equally strange that we can vividly recall a day five years ago in every lavish detail, yet we can't remember what we had for lunch yesterday? I know distances on linear planes might be a straight dash from one point of view to the next, but time still revolves in a closed circuit that has one preceding twelve with another kind of apostolic fervor and craze. Still, I assumed the mystery man to be Joe.

I took the spools and quickly settled into an isolated workstation in the rear of the library where I soon downloaded the first cartridge into a Series 8000 viewfinder. This primitive, clumsy device, although still serving a purpose, looked like an overweight anachronism[172]. To tell you the truth, it resembled an escapee from Joe's house more so than a piece of equipment owned by the City of Miami.

The small green screen suddenly burst to life with newspaper articles and corresponding photographs of a Nation on the brink of civil war. Everything shrunken like skulls to appease a headhunter's condensed format were now larger than life. This old technology, which somehow avoided that coup de grace[173] administered in the name of Progress, eventually relinquished itself to the task at hand. Only instead of manually turning page after monotonous page, I needed only to twist a well-worn plastic knob to beckon time both forward and back. With merely the flick of a wrist I could now circumvent days and weeks at a time.

I twisted and turned, zooming frantically past headlines and faces as a Nation mobilized from fighting words to fixed bayonets. On some subterranean level I had a sense of being there with those naïve volunteers who found themselves in battle but were missing in action all the same. I suppose Hell is always the same, regardless the time and place.

The menagerie on microfiche was a natural progression of man's macabre obsession that went from Cliff Notes in American History 101 to a crash course in knowing a little too much about minie balls[174], ironclads[175], and germ infested field hospitals where cleanliness was no more near Godliness than an atheist who wasn't stuffed in a foxhole.

I kept turning and turning restless as a man caught in a living nightmare. April fled to May, and May, like a lesbian lover, retreated into the warm arms of June. Columns of men and words dizzily raced past my portal as the winds of war stirred a nation to a frenzied pitch of hatred and nonstop bloodshed.

Winter to Spring to Summer to Fall, yet there was no defining winners or declaring losers after Bull Run. What, though, makes the fool?—The corner chair?—The pointed hat?—Or the belief that your God is an accomplice to genocide and murder?

September gave way to October and a second cartridge no different than the first. Body counts and the noble dead were the new royalty on the front page of every major newspaper. Blood, guts, and red badges[176] of courage littered every coronated battlefield, cornfield, and preliminary March to the Sea[177]. America was split apart yet beside herself. It was the perfect duality that accompanied acts of kindness amongst enemies on battlefields that were once brothers in arms.

Still, it didn't stop December from ushering in another year of conflict along the Mason-Dixon line[178]. Soon January melted into February, then March, which appeared with the roar of a lion and a dilatory pretender to the Little Corporal's[179] throne.

Photos were again taken just before the dead were collected as broken toys to be brought back to their original manufacturer. A twist here, a turn there, the Nones[180] led to the Ides[181] and to military operations, federal offensives, and General McClellan's[182] Peninsula campaign. Faces, places, and words slowly sifted across the verdant screen until I happened upon the 4th Balloon Regiment with Professor Lowe and a bearded bevy of soldiers and civilians.

Again I was brought back to flight. But of all the photos dedicated to Professor Lowe and the spy balloon Intrepid, only one by Brady was dated March 17, 1862. Beyond an elevated balloon in the background, however, nothing was exceptional about this particular photograph. To me, it looked like a dozen others with that expectant anomaly hovering in the subordinated rear. I'm not saying it was generic, but it was awfully familiar in composition and theme.

What made this photograph so important when it appeared so typical? That perplexed me to no end. It no more seemed worth killing over than dying for. Any lingering doubts I may have had about Joe removing this particular photo from his book were finally dispelled and laid to rest. The question of why it was removed, however, continued to annoy me. It wasn't for profit or monetary gain, that's for sure.—Then why? What was it about this insignificant photograph that made it the object of Joe's eyes as well as the person who ripped it out of a very expensive book?

After enlargement, which on a Series 8000 is only factor two, there was still no satisfactory resolution. Instead of distinguishing characteristics and features, the pixel clarity decreased exponentially[183]. There were no clean up features on this ancient technology either. That left me with one viable option: to request a print to download and enlarge on my computer at home. I finished the last spool mainly out of curiosity, but after Gettysburg in the summer of 1863 there was nothing in photo or print about balloons, rockoons, or Professor Lowe. It was as if he too just vanished from the pages of history.

CHAPTER NINE

2 Sides of the Story

THE EMPTINESS IN my house that night accompanied an emotional darkness artificially subjugated by the casual flip of a switch. Although no one had recently been killed there, a sense of loss prevailed nonetheless. What had perished did so long before my divorce from Karen was final. Love really never existed there as much as it clung to life support out of a parasitical need for blowjobs and frozen pizzas entombed in microwaves.

Pushing buttons and turning on my computer had become my main squeeze that I didn't have to wine and dine in order to get to second base. How far my checklist had been revised; I went from mounting big game trophies stuffed with blue point oysters to how to better nail the poster child for daddy issues in three easy lessons. Who, though, hasn't suffered as a casualty of love? The list is probably as long as those of any other war for independence. One in a million, after all, has as much to do with lightning strikes as it does lotteries and shark attacks outside pool halls in New Jersey.

After battening down the hatches for the night, I down-loaded the photo into my Apple Computer. For what reason though, I still had no idea. Remember, it wasn't what I was looking at but rather what Joe was looking for. I wasn't as preoccupied and curious, as I was bewitched. Despite the quaint method by which this photograph was originally conceived and brought to life in some now forgotten dark room, it still maintained a stark contrast that although limited in colorful anecdote nevertheless defined traits, quirks, and other physical idiosyncrasies exclusive to that moment in time crystallized a one-hundred and fifty-eight years before.

Besides the scene-stealing balloon, there were thirty-three men grouped around Professor Lowe with his slightly cocked stovepipe hat. However, no other man was listed by name, rank, or civilian trademark. It was Professor Lowe and everybody else on his field staff, so obtaining any sort of personal information was impossible to collect and ascertain. Upon cleaning and magnification, some men were so overrun with scraggy beards that all that was discernible were their beady eyes. Biblical patriarchs had nothing on these hirsute[184] specimens. Wide brimmed hats also attributed to that scourge of incognito that could not be remedied regardless how many times I digitally enhanced the photo.

Deposing one man and exorcising another became a process of elimination in a field populated with high hopes and noxious[185] weed. I went slowly down the line, back to front, right to left, preening, ferreting, and trying to desperately see what Joe might have been looking for, other than the obvious. What, though, did these bearded trolls[186] have in common other than a bridge, a union card, and an age-old desire to fly?

I never agonized over one photo. I scrutinized every last feature and detail of every single person and object. I could eliminate some people and things right from the start. But, as the straining increased and became hard pressed, more and more succumbed to join those others disqualified by shadow, positioning, or lack of focal perspective.

What caught my eye, however, was a young civilian man standing to the immediate right of Professor Lowe. He was at once all-too-familiar and someone I couldn't yet put a finger on. Not only was this young man the tallest; he was also the only one who had a keloid[187] on his lightly fleeced face. Could this by chance be the "SCAR" Joe alluded to in his book? But why would a crab's claw[188] on a man's face from the Civil War warrant mention in the margin of a very expensive book?

I zoomed in until the young man's face filled the computer screen. Clearer, nearer the keepsake swelled in measure and all points' bulletin scale. I was mesmerized by not only a face in the crowd, but also a very familiar face. It soon congealed into a prolonged staring contest that forever eliminated those who blinked first.

What are the odds of two people having the same twenty-six facial regions and vertical properties? And the same exact token of remembrance on the same temple? Scars, like fingerprints, are incriminating things reserved for one's exclusiveness of being intimate but never dear. Was it coincidence? Perhaps a fluke, like a snowflake that has a doppelgänger[189] with another story to tell about uniqueness and individuality?

Then the realization of it hit me. This wasn't about early manned flight, Professor Lowe, or the Civil War. It was about photos—photos of Dick Sanders! "I'll be damned," I gasped in disbelief as the two faces morphed into one signature revelation that now made perfect sense in a not-so-perfect world.

"Now you know how we feel Mr. Moore," a stranger's voice dorsally sliced the murky den.

If I hadn't been so exhausted and in a state of shock I might have responded differently to this intruder's clipped, yet familiar voice. Still, I was propelled to my feet. But if I was startled before it was only a prelude to what was to follow when I turned to see who had the drop on me.

"Sit, Sit," Thomas Webster commanded after materializing from the menacing shadows brandishing a pug nosed 38. "Just couldn't leave well enough alone, could you? I guess what your friend Joe told you about Dick doesn't really matter anymore. All that matters now is who you told," Tom inquired as Harry Collins and Dick Sanders now crossed that demarcation line between shadow and substance.

"Joe didn't say anything to me," I vehemently protested.

"Yours was the last number he called that night," Harry entered the verbal fray that was more an interrogation than a friendly Q&A.

"All Joe said was he had something to tell me. But in regards to who or what, he wouldn't divulge over an unsecured line," I set the phone record straight.

"What are we waiting for? Kill him!" Dick nervously prattled.

"So it's true, you are the one in the photograph," I accused. A guilty nod by Dick confirmed what I still couldn't believe. "But how?" I rhetorically muttered.

"To think we've been here all these years and it was one innocuous photo that almost tripped us up; it boggles the mind," Tom conceded.

"What do you want? I told you I don't know anything," I cut to the quick.

"Now, now, Mr. Moore. Don't be so melodramatic for even ignorance is temporary," Tom calmly reassured.

"We have to kill him, he knows too much," Harry seconded.

"But he might serve our purposes yet." Tom championed my stay of execution.

"You can't be serious! Him?" Harry sneered.

"Why not? After tonight, we'll be on launch lockdown so it's now or never," Tom implied.

"I suppose we could do worse," Dick reluctantly agreed.

"He's better than some kook from a trailer park," Tom remarked.

"Or some nutty Professor," Harry sarcastically blurted.

"What other choice do we have? Our situation is what it is," Tom contended.

"But we always said it should be a dedicated man of science," Dick reminded.

"The truth is the truth, regardless of whose mouth it falls from," Tom countered.

"But can we trust him?" Harry thrust a lanky figure in my direction.

"Men who deal in facts believe in truth, isn't that right Mr. Moore?" Tom spoke on my stunned behalf.

"What do you want from me?" I testily argued as a man who hadn't slept in over three days.

"We want you to tell our story," Tom matter-of-factly disclosed.

"I don't understand. What story?" I quizzically asked.

"Our story, your story, the World's story," Dick enigmatically tossed. "Take your pick."

"You have to understand as we're victims of circumstance, so, in essence, you are too, Mr. Moore," Tom correlated the common denominator.

"It's hard to be called a victim when you're holding a gun," I promptly surmised.

"Only a necessary evil," Tom apologized as he lowered the menacing weapon to his side.

"What other choice do I have?" I half asked.

"Between ignorance and knowledge or life and death, neither I'm afraid," Tom bluntly summed up my tenuous predicament.

After several more minutes of verbal shuttlecock between Tom, Dick and Harry and myself, I finally agreed to the conditions and terms laid down by Tom, which basically consisted of living to see another day or dying right there on the spot. I was, needless to say, scared for my life. I remembered from Survival School that you have to placate a man with a gun. At the time, I still didn't know what to make of the situation or my status. Hell, I didn't even know what to make of Tom Webster, Dick Sanders or Harry Collins for that matter. A million things were racing through my mind at once, foremost being to stay alive regardless the cost. Quite frankly, I was really no different from that proverbial horny guy in the backseat at the drive-in; only I was looking to get lucky in an entirely whole other way.

"What I'm about to tell you has never been heard by another human being, so listen carefully Mr. Moore, and please try not to interrupt because I only have time to say this but once," Tom imparted.

"We come from a planetary system in the Constellation Hercules[190] that by Earth's calculations is twenty-four thousand light years[191] away," Tom commenced in earnest after taking a seat next to my computer station. "With a crew of eleven and me at the Captain's helm, we were sent out by our Planetary Governing Council to map out and fertilize neighboring solar systems for future colonization. But we were not just flag waving explorers; we were what you might call seeders, jump starters, evolutionary biologists versed in the Universal Building Blocks of DNA. Our mission was to pave the way for future colonization by engineering life forms on select planets in order to achieve biodiversity and climate stability."

"Everything was going routinely and according to schedule until the 19th Celestial Cycle," Tom disclosed. "Then, without warning, our mother ship was bombarded by a massive meteor shower between

Ophiuchus and Scorpius[192] where the red monster Antares[193] rules supreme. Nine of my crew was killed instantly. The three of us also sustained injuries, but none as severe and life-threatening as Dick's head wound."

"Never had we encountered a meteor storm of this magnitude. Not only were we injured; our vessel was damaged beyond repair. What made our situation more dire was that all primary and secondary communication systems were neutralized by electromagnetic particles that infiltrated the command module. So not only were we crippled, we were also incapable of transmitting even the most basic of distress signal. It's not as if we were just a few leagues from home, we were half a parsec[194] from the nearest colonial trading post in Ara[195]."

"In addition to that, the ship's nuclear core was compromised and gradually spewing plutonium," Tom continued. "With no functional gyroscopes navigational control was for all intent and purposes limited to full speed ahead. We were hurtling through uncharted deep space at Elemental Level 29, three times the optimal speed of hyper optic velocity, approximately six million miles per hour. In this reckless injured state, we timelessly drifted through wormholes not knowing where we were going except further and further from our beloved world where the average lifespan is equivalent to a hundred thousand solar years."

"We traveled for centuries in this incapacitated condition until we crash landed in what is now modern day France. Although we survived the fiery impact, most of our technical and scientific instruments did not. Unfortunately the Earth we were shipwrecked upon is not the same one we know and sing praises of today. The world of thirty thousand years ago was a cold, dark, primitive world—a world we knew all too well from our "seeding missions" throughout the Universe."

"At the time of our arrival, both the Neanderthal and Cro-Magnon species were half-ape and still fixated with things made of crude stone," Tom attested. "It was as if we were held hostage in a time warp. We couldn't have asked for a more backwater boondock to be deserted upon. Don't get me wrong, we were happy to be alive; we just weren't happy to be here, wherever the hell here was."

"What was equally troubling was the fact that we couldn't blend into our new environment that, despite an extra molecule of hydrogen, is nearly identical to the atmosphere on our planet that as our names cannot be translated into English. I believe it is the presence of this additional molecule that has glacially retarded our aging process," Tom diagnosed.

"We were the exact opposite of everything these ape men were, only we represented the other extreme of not only new, but different."

"Our introduction was a mixed reception. If we weren't looked upon as fire bringers from the heavens then we were looked upon as members of a rival cave clan. This later perception never changed. It was the same before as it was after we discarded our spacesuits and adopted the local dress. But even then we couldn't hide the fact we were innately different. Not only were we white and erect, we weren't carpeted in mats of knotty, smelly fur, emblematic of both humanoid species at the time."

"It took years and many trinkets to garner trust and acceptance with these primitive savages. Really, what else did we have? All we had in abundance was time; time to think, time to plan, time to dream. In that vein we were richer than Croesus[196]. It was the only luxury we had besides our field test kits that we were able to salvage from our ship's wreckage. Basic and fundamental yes, but with these tools we could design and genetically engineer a better species of man."

"We were only doing what we were trained to do," Tom added, "the difference being we would now have to seed as well as cultivate and harvest our bounty. It was opposed to everything we ever did in good faith or sound science. We had no choice but to be hands on every minute of every day. Many were the hurdles, foremost being a common form of communication other than grunts, groans, and excessive finger pointing, another of man's bad habits that started long before we got here."

"We were ignorant of this alien world as we were its indigenous life forms. We knew from the outset that in order to succeed we would require a solid foundation that could be built upon from generation to generation. Laying down concrete infrastructures was only part of the problem; we also had to plant abstract embryos. It's not to say we weren't up to the challenge, it's just that neither species of man was ready to learn quantum physics any more than basic math. We knew we would eventually have to make a decision and stand. In a two horse race it leaves no room for error or second guesses."

"We toiled for years, doing extensive research and running batteries of tests to see which species would be more suitable for the traits we wanted to genetically isolate and expound upon. We finally decided to put all our energy and tools in the Cro-Magnon line. Make no mistake, Neanderthals had many favorable attributes and qualities, it's just they had great difficulty with even the most basic of spatial concepts. And we just couldn't allow that boorishness to seep into the Genome Model."

"In retrospect, our decision only hastened an evolutionary process. The outcome between these two archrivals was determined long before we happened upon the ancient landscape. But even after we declared a winner for hunting grounds and waterholes, there still was much to do, including establishing permanent and electrical connections in the cerebral cortex. You just don't hand savages typewriters and expect them to hammer out the "Great Gatsby.""

"We still had to build the modern prototype of man, which soon became our number one priority. You see Mr. Moore," Tom admitted, "there is no missing link in man's family tree; we just bumped man up a rung on the evolutionary ladder. But that jump from half ape to all man, was necessary for our survival and very existence. Simply put, we had to make apes in our image so we could blend into our new, alien environment. That, however, was only the first step. We still had to design a sophisticated race of man who could help us build a spaceship. But we couldn't have one without the other."

"As with all educational curriculums it was beset by trial and error. We couldn't help it, but as we taught we learned more and more about the dual nature of man. Overcoming customary approaches to solving problems was difficult to diffuse and short-circuit from the very beginning. Long before our earthly ministry began, the fear of the unknown was already well established in man's electrical conduits. In some instances, inroads were so deeply seated we couldn't dig deep enough to uproot their imprint. Nothing we tried succeeded; trepanning[197], lobotomies, grafting[198], nothing could reverse that discharge in the hippocampus, which we later distilled was chemical in origin."

"In the beginning we wanted knowledge to be rewarding and user-friendly. We wanted to leave wiggle room for individual temperament and interpretation. We wanted knowledge to be a harbinger of flexible guidelines, not a repressive regime of crossed t's and dotted i's," Tom announced.

"The last thing we wanted to do was to discourage early man with information overload. We gave early man many gifts, including flint, fire, and the wheel. But just when he was beginning to understand his abilities and play with his new toys, he was in the grips of death. On average, man's meager lifespan lasted three decades, which was another major stumbling block we couldn't yet overcome medically or genetically."

"Man's longevity was paramount to everything we were trying to instill and accomplish. Just when we were beginning to tap into a student's potential he would be teetering on the cusp of mortality. The opportunities afforded us were so brief, sometimes a few months, barely long enough to teach a man much of anything, including what's right and wrong."

"We tended and nursed our flocks as they went from sooty caves to grassy plains. We were vigilant in charting man's physical and mental development. Through autopsies, we observed this anatomical progression. As anxious stewards, we watched as man's brain doubled in size and mass, testament to our scientific capabilities of stoking those creative fires without having to first rub two sticks together under the tented pretext of a religious fly-by-night revival. This feat of genetic engineering was accomplished within eight thousand years," Tom proudly beamed. "We knew from our Planet's anthropological record that entails roughly seven-hundred and fifty million Earth years that to successfully bring a savage people to a technically advanced Super State takes a thousand generations, which to us was nine-hundred and ninety-nine generations too long."

"It's only natural for inpatient parents to hurry their kids out the front door. We were no different. The only way to accomplish this was by tinkering with the Double Helix[199]. Our circumventions, like most shortcuts, didn't always bring about the desired results. The freak show, it is said, only begins in the womb," Tom asserted. "We never knew what was going to pop out of that Jack-in-the-Box. Would it be sickly, monstrous, or would the baby batter be just right? Even with the right tools under proper conditions, it was still a crapshoot and guessing game for nine months. Still, we can't be held responsible for freaks of nature when they were already prisoners in the cells of man."

"During good times and bad, we oversaw our flocks and their activities that were gradually becoming more complex and sophisticated. Man was on the move in every direction in every land. More importantly, he was carrying languages and tools that were no longer made of crude stone. We remained in ancient France until our security blanket could no longer keep us warm from the ever advancing Ice Age," Tom recounted. "We migrated southeast with several hundred of our most gifted students to escape the bitter cold and to inaugurate a new kind of Learning Center that would revolutionize thought."

"Atlantis was no myth, no fabled land, Mr. Moore, it was our brainchild, our diamond in the atavistic[200] rough," Tom proclaimed. "What started as a pre-Lyceum[201] classroom in the garden of Apollo seven-thousand years ago grew into a Mediterranean power that had no rival. The island was so sacred and special that the gods of Olympus were born there. For the first time in our Earthly ministry, everything was aligned and in harmony. We had the right climate, the perfect island, and the ideal student body upon whose shoulders we could proudly stand upon as we clawed our way back into the heavens."

"Physics, Geometry, Chemistry, and Astronomy were just some of the advanced subjects taught on Atlantis. But Atlantis was more than a school of higher learning. It was also a testing ground for all types of experiments. With our guidance our students invented microscopes, telescopes, metallurgy, aqualungs, and the concept of zero. The thousands of machines and mechanical devices created and produced on Atlantis would not be surpassed until the latter decades of the 20ᵗʰ century. Atlantis was more than a technocracy; however, it also laid at the center of a vast flourishing trade network in the Mediterranean."

"In all our earthly years, we were never more content as we were on Atlantis. We had no meddlesome governments, no religious vendettas, or internecine wars. It was a special time, a special place, the likes of which your world will never see again."

"But all good things must come to an end," Tom sorrowfully disclosed. "All our work, all our sacrifice went for naught when a volcano on the Isle of Thera exploded in the Aegean Sea. The greatest volcanic eruption the world had ever heard wiped out the most gifted students the world would never know. In a moment's rage a cataclysmic wall of water consumed Atlantis, swallowing her whole. Poof! Just like that, she was gone forever."

"In all our sentenced days, we were never as close to death as we were that morning. As luck would have it, we were conducting underwater experiments. The only reason we were survivors and not victims from a population of twenty-five thousand strong. This deadly deluge, the progenitor of all flood stories from Gilgamesh[202] to Noah, not only killed our most gifted pupils, it destroyed our library. Atlantis was our first concerted effort at warehousing the written word. On our Planet, there's no longer a need for teaching materials. Our students only have to hear something once to understand its meaning, unlike man, who has to see it, read it, and have it drummed ad nauseum[203] into his head. The literary loss at Atlantis would not be replaced for another five-thousand years until our Library at Alexandria, which met its earthly demise at the opposite extreme of 'water, water everywhere'."

"Our laboratories and, more importantly, the scientific tools of our trade, including that which we were able to salvage from our ship, were also destroyed. Now everything from our world was gone, some things forever, other things until the advent of the Space Age. We were this close to the perfect man, this close," Tom regretfully narrowed his forefinger and thumb. "Left with no scientific instruments we were now powerless to improve man's genetic lot."

"After Atlantis we thought we were doomed to spend the remainder of our days on Earth. Disappointment was more than a password for our living hell. If a man spends eight hours a day for thirty years doing something, whatever it is, it seems like an eternity. Now imagine twenty-two thousand years working for that same standard and gold watch. We learned a valuable lesson from this catastrophe: never put all your eggheads in one basin."

"It wasn't a total loss; significant remnants survived the drowning of Atlantis. Being a seafaring island, Atlantis spread its thought and language from the Levant[204] to Maghreb[205]. All Indo-European languages, including Sanskrit, have their comparative roots in this now forgotten trade vernacular. Never again would we have such influence of subject and medium as we did on Atlantis. It was our once-in-a-lifetime opportunity."

"The human population after the deluge was rapidly expanding and advancing into regions once ruled by the emperors of ice. Man was also beginning to experiment with permanent settlements in and around Jericho[206]. Religions that would subsequently prove to be our biggest competitors for the hearts and minds of men were also beginning to take shape."

"After the death of Atlantis, we carried torches into many dark and distant lands. This was our final prolonged ministry of spreading seeds and planting roots. For over four-thousand years we converted and proselytized[207] people to our way of thinking about escape plans. However, we no longer did so in the capacity of ward and protector of man's sperm and affairs. We were as lightning rods trying to enlighten man. Our ministry took us to Asia, Africa, and back to Europe. We were as lust-ridden Lothario's[208] dispersing our seeds into as many fertile minds as possible. It might have been a different strategy but it was the same story. We wanted to plant seeds so thoughts could grow as magic beans."

"Eventually we returned to Athens where we had earlier washed ashore with a thousand corpses[209]," Tom gloomily recalled. "Athens was no longer a fishing village with Bronze Age men dreaming of distant shores. Now it was a city replete with schools, teachers, and curiosity. Our seeds had grown way beyond our expectations. In this Golden Age, we had no shortage of students or enthusiastic followers to our version of reaching for the stars. Again, we could adjust and focus eyes beyond the horizon. We could again guide thoughts to a greater audience for discussion and debate. Next to the Atlanteans, the Greeks were our favorite pupils. They were such a quick study. It was a pleasure to discuss our travel itinerary with these exceptional thinkers. Democritus[210] believed in the existence of atoms and dark matter before we met him in Athens, where he practiced what he preached as if it was Gospel according to Tom, Dick and Harry."

"Above all else, the Greeks understood cause-and-effect. They equally knew the importance of observation and extrapolation[211]. They were proficient at projecting knowledge into spheres they knew existed, but not on any conventional map of the Aegean. At one time or another, our classrooms held Solon, Phidias, Aristophanes, Hippocrates, Euripides, Plato, and Socrates, our first martyr. Dick here," Tom pointed out, "privately tutored the young Alexander the Great before passing the mental baton onto my former student Aristotle."

"As with all our students, whether Pericles, Pythagoras or Archimedes, we gave each a special gift they could re-wrap and present to man under his collective Tree of Knowledge. It wouldn't be the first or last time our students would be bestowed with laurels and accolades and be called geniuses with their special understanding of knowledge from out of this world. We stood off in the wings as proud parents allowing our brainchildren to indulge in vanity's spotlight. We knew we couldn't raise fulcrums any more than a sculpture's chisel. Instead, we found sanctuary in anonymity, which would become a timeless theme. It's not to say we weren't tempted," Tom sadly confessed.

"The trappings of success are very enticing when toiling in obscurity and living hand to mouth. Yet we fastened ourselves to the yoke of poverty that didn't draw attention to anything save more flies. Besides, no fame or fortune could compensate us for what was truly missing in our lives."

"For the longest time, humble pie was our main staple. We even gave the Wright brothers, bicycle mechanics by trade, the credit for the first powered flight at Kitty Hawk. Imagine that," Tom marveled, "bicycle mechanics! Yet they insist the Christian God works in mysterious ways."

"After Greece was absorbed in the Pax Romano[212], we migrated up the cradle of civilization to Rome where we found another willing yet very different kind of bumper crop," Tom continued. "The Romans were crafty and aggressive. Their minds were predisposed to violence. This was yet another reptilian trait we couldn't uproot and eradicate from man's genetic profile. At the time all roads led to Rome, including ours. But we always had to go where the iron was hottest. Their legions provided the way for the flowering of culture and the written word, two things that interested us a great deal. Whoever would have thought bloodletting would be the vital fluid to nourish our Tree of Knowledge? This Roman holiday[213] was no picnic. Rome proved you could advance troops and wisdom at the expense of human suffering."

"We tutored everyone from children of senators to slaves. No one actually knows where a brilliant mind is going to spring up with the Muses[214]. Great men can be born in log cabins just as easily as castles. Wherever students were open and inclined was where we went to preach the Gospel of Physics."

"We remained in the Roman Empire for almost five centuries. Caesar, Cicero, and Pliny the Elder were our chief students that history still knows to this day. The Romans were astute thinkers, but they were much too practical when it came to things beyond the jurisdiction of Rome. They had no intellectual curiosity to rival the Greeks. They even stole their gods and gave them new names. What do you expect when people are first trained to fight then taught how to spell their name?"

"It was only after Attila sacked Rome that we parted company with these debauched descendents of Nero. We again became itinerants wandering from town to town. We stayed primarily in Western Europe during the Dark Ages, where, ironically, the flame of knowledge was maintained by monks in monasteries, those lighthouses in the Sea of

Ignorance. We didn't set foot back in Italy until the Renaissance, when man again created beauty and wonder out of lifeless stone. Flying under the radar disguised, as poor teachers didn't preclude us from charges of heresy. The Roman Inquisition leveled charges against me and my student Galileo, who after being placed under house arrest by Pope Urban VIII, was never publicly seen again."

"Charges of sorcery, witchcraft, and blasphemy hectored every man of learning who went against the grain of Christianity. Italy has always been a land of two extremes. Where else could you find St. Peter and Commodus? Our gift of zymurgy[215] may have been sweet, but its juices all flowed from sour and bitter grapes."

"Our vagabond appearances may have stayed the same over the years, but our teaching methods were in a constant state of flux. We had to be cognizant of political climates and religious intolerances all throughout Europe. Sometimes we led our students by example, other times we just sat back and watched from the rear of the theater. Some things, however, we just couldn't leave to chance or conjecture. Our lives depended on us making sure Science didn't backslide and revert to alchemy[216] or worse, the black arts. When scholarly debate stalled, we jump-started the discussion with key papers anonymously submitted to select scientists and professors. For twenty-three years Isaac Newton was our liaison and middleman to those cathedrals of higher learning[217] throughout Europe."

"Even then some truths got lost in translation. Men of knowledge can't be startled from their prejudices. They also have to gradually be awoken from their stupor so to not chase them from the light. Knowledge should never scare people. It's counterproductive as all love affairs on dead-end streets. Sometimes slow and steady is the only way to prove a point."

"During the Age of Enlightenment we were never far removed from campus life. It was imperative for us to be near those shrines dedicated to the Laws of Motion and Cartesian[218] Coordinates. We also had to be aware of the next generation of scientists, mathematicians, inventors, professors, and philosophers."

"What was beginning to interest us by the 18th century was America. We heard many inspiring stories about those revolutionary firebrands and radical thinkers who incorporated freedom of speech, happiness, and religion into their National Charter. We knew we had to take our light show across the pond[219]. The freshness of rebel minds unspoiled by stuffy traditions and stale ways of thought was too much for us to resist. The nice thing was that we could go to America and not worry about another Dark Ages tearing up our Tree of Knowledge."

"Once again, we departed our designated home away from home in France to begin our final ministry. When we arrived in Philadelphia in 1794 we were not disappointed. We found Americans industrious, engaging, and forever looking to build a better mousetrap. They also thought on a grand scale, even when they didn't have a pot to piss in. Still that didn't discourage them from dreaming big. That's what put them in good steed with us," Tom illuminated, "to not only have broad shoulders, but broad minds. For us it was the best of both possible worlds. We sounded Americans every chance we could. We never encountered Americans or the New World so it was not only terra nova[220] physically, but mentally."

"Unlike Europe, common people in America could aspire to higher office and travel in higher circles. It didn't matter what a man had in his pocket, but what he had in his head. It was a refreshing reversal. Not since Atlantis had we this much intellectual freedom. How rewarding it was for us to see our teachings that we put in motion thousands of years earlier, crossing oceans, languages, and cultures. In America, our seeds found application in many bold and daring new forms in science and industry. Some innovations we could see coming down the assembly line, others we had no idea such things were possible. That was the remarkable thing about Americans; they had active imaginations that never genuflected before the altar of practicality."

"They utilized abstracts, not as intangibles, but as a way of thinking about life beyond borders and cries of Westward ho! Americans were unique, they were aggressive like the Romans, even taking the eagle as their battle standard, but they were thinkers in the same mold and mindset as the Greeks. At first it might seem an unlikely combination, but in reality it only showcases the duality of man's nature."

"Over the years we discussed life with everyone from Jefferson and Franklin, to Fulton and Edison. We even befriended a young and impressionable Robert Goddard, the father of the modern rocket."

"But just as in Europe, we had to keep moving to avoid detection. Despite every precaution, the world can still be a very small place. Crossing paths with people we had met decades earlier has happened more often than I care to admit," Tom reluctantly alluded. "You can see the awkwardness of the situation. Having not aged a day put us in league with the devil. And we all know what that means. Out of necessity, we had to keep moving as the Great White[221] to stay alive."

"After photography was introduced in the 1840s, all our Washington social circles dried up. We couldn't take the chance of revolving around men we made famous. We never knew when one of those shutterbugs would show up with their spindly tripods. Who was to know Dick's courting of Professor Lowe would almost prove to be our undoing? That hard head of my brother's has been as much a blessing as a curse, costing many a man his life."

"Like Joe," I indignantly chimed, breaking my self-imposed silence.

"We had no other choice," Tom petitioned.

"What about Campbell and Snyder?" I hurriedly snapped.

"We came together and we're going to leave together," Tom recited a brotherly oath sworn to three-hundred centuries earlier. "It's the least we expect for services rendered. You can't deny us that, no human can. In relation to the lives we've saved, the ones we've sacrificed are insignificant by comparison."

"Significant, insignificant, it's still murder," I dutifully barked.

"Forgive me, Mr. Moore," Tom quickly apologized, "I'm not trying to underscore your anger or your loss. All I'm saying is that some sort of gratitude should be afforded us. We deserve it, and not just because we're homesick and late for dinner."

"Think of it as payback, as quid pro quo[222]," Dick commented.

"How about I call it first degree murder and leave it at that?" I turned the sacrificial altar.

"You're forgetting one very important thing," Tom reminded. "Without us, man would still be playing with rocks and wondering if the moon were made of green cheese. Granted, some inventions would have been independently created by some fool screaming 'Eureka'. But then, of course, everything looks easy to do after it's been explained, copyrighted and mass-produced."

"Without our periodic intervention and generous gift giving, there would've been no Thales, Euclid, Heron, Galen, DaVinci, Copernicus, Brahe, Descartes, Newton, Huygens, Von Braun, Alder, Hubble, Teller, Hawking, Hale, or Einstein, our favorite patent clerk," Tom rattled a chain of who's who. "All those giants of science and technology would have remained mental midgets reduced to living memory and the impersonal nothingness of mortal dust that has no historical roll call. How do you suppose mankind went from Kitty Hawk[233] to the Sea of Tranquility[224] in just a few decades? We, Mr. Moore," Tom circled the trio, "we propelled and dragged man into space, not only to see but to see for himself."

"So what you're telling me is that despite being exceptional, you're the rule nonetheless," I paraphrased.

"There is always entitlement for the empowered," Tom correlated. "Victors have been butchering losers long before we arrived upon this earthly battlefield."

"Remember, Mr. Moore," Harry chirped, "gods and generals require no malpractice insurance. It's a well-known fact that where there's sheep, there's slaughterhouses."

"I didn't know how any of this was going to transpire, none of us did," Tom related. "We are many things, Mr. Moore, but we are not fortune tellers. It was new for us too, both in application and theory, and just like earthlings, we became creatures by accident and relative design."

"Still, it's not right, not to mention anything of it being fair," I retorted, as the hair on my neck bristled in anger and disgust.

"Fair, fair," Tom angrily spewed. "If things were fair, Campbell and Snyder would still be alive today. A corrupt, bloated system killed them long before we did."

"But you're not gods," I indignantly accused.

"Not in the omnipotent sense," Tom split proper nouns. "Still, we're creators and bringers of light who fell from the heavens."

"Prometheus[225] be damned," Dick jealously recanted.

"You forget Lucifer also fell from the heavens," I defiantly sounded.

"Apples and oranges, nothing more," Harry side barred.

"Being deserving because you expect it is a little too self serving if you ask me," I righteously harped.

"The only problem with that, Mr. Moore, is nobody is asking you," Tom imparted a disclaimer. "We don't need permission from you or anybody else for that matter. It would be like asking a two-year-old for the keys to the family auto."

"But it's all been a lie, a charade, a hoax, everything," I fervently admonished.

"You don't necessarily have to be imprisoned for the truth to set you free," Tom pointed out.

"How, though, can the average man come to terms with that bone of contention," I reinforced an older ignorance. "You forget people believe man was made in God's image on the Sixth Day."

"Revolutionary change is always a nasty business," Tom disclosed, "whether beheading tyrants or ridding oneself of preconceived notions. Slaying monsters is, after all, in the eye of the beholder, Mr. Moore."

"The only problem with that is when you're going home I just won't be fighting prejudices, but rather thousands of years of traditions and rituals." I spotted the fly in the alien ointment. "For me it's a lose-lose proposition. And I don't care who's holding the cards or carrying the body bag of man."

"The phoenix will never rise from the ashes of ignorance if the truth, the real truth, remains untold," Tom countered.

"That's easy for you to say," I persisted, "but I'll be the one torpedoing gods and national heroes. What's more, I'll be branded, labeled a kook, a nut, an iconoclastic crackpot. And what will I have to support these outrageous allegations and slanderous claims? Your precious word, oh yeah, and a Civil War photo of Dick here or whatever the fuck his name is."

"So you think people are happiest when they're ignorant, barefoot and out of the loop," Tom queried.

"No, all I'm trying to impress upon you is the fact that people will not accept this at face value," I jabbed the frozen computer screen that held the credentials of yesterday and today.

"I'll grant you that, Mr. Moore. Faith nowadays requires mortar and bricks," Tom agreed in principle. "But by your own admission, salesmanship has more to do with presentation than the product itself."

"All I'm saying is if you want me to do your spade work and bidding I'll need something a little more substantial and concrete. Something that can't be refuted, disputed or turned around to mean something else entirely," I upped the ante.

"Our spaceship is located 47 degrees longitude, 3 degrees latitude, approximately seventeen-hundred yards southwest of the pre-historic caves in Auvergne, France," Tom revealed a thirty-thousand year-old secret.

"I still don't know if I can turn the world upside down. Discoverers and whistle blowers are known by other names too, depending on which side of the Atlantic they're originally from," I appealed giving voice to my ever growing doubts.

"Too much information, not enough. Mr. Moore, your problem has no easy answers. Even when you think you know all the questions," Tom glibly chastised.

"Sometimes slash and burn tactics are the only way to get people's attention. That's something to remember, Mr. Moore," Dick quickly intervened, before disappearing back into the shadows of his older brother.

"Like St. Michaels in Chicago," I sent a salvo across the alien bow.

"Just another necessary evil, nothing more," Tom retaliated.

"Is that why you butchered Joe?" I hurriedly surveyed their stoic faces.

"What better way to cover our tracks?" Tom admitted his culpability. "If you act like a deranged madman the police will be looking for one. It was only another misdirection ploy. We, after all, just couldn't shoot your friend Joe any more than Campbell and Snyder. We had to make their deaths so heinous that no one would ever suspect us."

"Who would ever suspect our All-American fly boys at NASA?" I sarcastically mocked the messenger's apparent contradiction in terms.

"Just your friend Joe," Tom intimated. "Only he approached me with his reservations about Dick. Why he confided to me that day in the cafeteria at NASA I still don't know. Maybe to provoke a reaction on the subject."

"What subject?" I curiously picked up the scent.

"Time travel," Tom divulged.

"But he was doing his job," I adversarially pursued.

"And we ours," Tom steadfastly maintained. "It was nothing personal if that's any consolation."

"How can I not take the killing of my best friend personally?" I fumed.

"In our fight to get back home, we've killed many people who were just doing their jobs," Tom coldly confessed.

"So basically what you're telling me is Joe was killed over a stupid Civil War photo," I persisted.

"I'm afraid it's a little more complicated than that," Tom elucidated. "Your friend Joe thought my brother to be a time traveler, a practice outlawed on our planet millions of years ago due to the potential transference of deadly pathogens along the space-time continuum. You might say your friend, Mr. Moore, was the last known casualty of the Civil War," Tom duly noted. "We just couldn't let all those years of waiting for this particular moment and the right three orphans to be in vain," Tom informed.

"Whom I'm sure you also conveniently silenced after assuming their identities," I euphemistically incriminated.

"You have to remember, in loose ends they tie hangman's knots," Tom rebutted.

"I know it's difficult under these extraordinary circumstances to put our plight into proper perspective, being your life span is so brief in relation to ours. But imagine, if you will, waiting on some dark, strange corner for seventy years for a ride home in a vehicle that doesn't yet exist on the 'Big Three's[226]' drawing board" Tom lectured.

Rummage that around before passing judgment on us," Harry intervened.

"Now, now," Tom diplomatically patted the electrified air. "This is not about who's right or who's wrong, who's living or who's dead.

We did our time, Mr. Moore, and now it's time for us to go home. We are living proof that the execution is never as painful as the wait to dawn."

"Come on! You know damn well you can't change truth like dirty oil after it's served its purpose," I reasoned.

"Everything, as everyone, is recyclable, including and especially gods," Tom emphasized.

"But to be the official whistle blower and biographer of mass murderers—how can I live with myself or die in peace, for that matter?" I guiltily burst.

"Just more mutable ethics," Tom exposed the flesh of this commercial trade.

"What that truth is not only painful, but deadly," I reinforced my battle line in the sand.

"Mr. Moore, your problem is you went in search of a truth you weren't ready to accept any more than embrace," Tom chastised. "Even now, as you confront it, you still hem and haw like a frightened little child. Truth has shades to be sure, but only man puts on rose tinted ones."

"It just seems so callous and cavalier to destroy all those illusions and myths you created and fostered over the course of history, that's all I'm saying," I cautiously maintained.

"You forget societies are nothing more than sand castles reinforced with steel and concrete," Tom mused.

"So that's it? You giveth, you taketh away," I defiantly persisted.

"Nothing is to last forever," Tom grimly reported. "Is, inevitably becomes Was. Time is just the final arbiter of this universal curfew. Just remember, life is all about adjustments, Mr. Moore. Each and every day you get out of bed your perspective is different in some way, shape or form. The angle by which you view life is constantly changing whether kneeling or sitting on a high horse."

"This is a lot to not only swallow, but digest. Killing anything is a lot for any man to stomach," I loudly mused, almost indifferent to my captors' presence.

"We may have given Democritus the knowledge of the atom, but it was Oppenheimer[227] who laid claim to being a destroyer of worlds," Tom imparted. "The facts are sometimes the hardest things to keep straight. In a way, I suppose they're like disoriented sots, only without street poles to cling to. So, measuring us by your moral barometers is ludicrous, if not ridiculous. We, after all, have a thirty thousand year advantage and head start that can't be changed by either grandfather clauses[228] or Domesticated Bulls[229]. Besides, we created man's internal and external script but it was never designed to include us. In a sense, we were as independent directors working on our own pet project."

"You're directors alright. Funeral directors," I sarcastically rebuked.

"But what do they decorate generals for—making friends or killing enemies?" Tom disclosed. "What I'm trying to impress upon you, Mr. Moore, is that we also had to change and adapt. We always had to compensate for man's duality of kill or be killed. Long ago, we discovered necessity and self-interest eliminated all other options.

"Still, it doesn't exonerate any of you unless murder is acceptable on your planet of birth," I reproached.

"Do you actually think any of us will ever go back to being who we were before we crashed here?" Tom flared. "We come from a world where murder and war, like treachery and deceit, are non-existent. None of us will ever be considered or mistaken for the entity we once were. Man's propensity for sudden, unprovoked violence put an unpredictability in our lives that we were never quite able to integrate or fully understand. You might say we never knew who or what else we were getting in the bargain and arrangement."

"I guess you still don't," I growled.

"We never did before, so why should it change now?" Tom admonished.

"You just make it sound so goddamn glib and self righteously convenient, that's all," I cynically yelped.

"None of us can be proud of every act and deed we've done in our lives," Tom professed. "We never claimed to be saints."

"Only gods," I snapped.

"But gods who didn't have to be nickel and dimed to death on Sundays," Tom clarified.

"I know. You did what you had to do. It's a tired refrain," I snorted a Nazi line that also killed millions.

"We owe no debt to any man or nation," Tom heralded.

"Only explanations to first causes and blood lines that stretch light years away," I inserted the caveat.

"That's where you come in, Mr. Moore," Tom diligently notified.

"But I will be reviled whether I walk in the front door or sneak around the back," I snarled at the proposition imposed upon me.

"Truth never claimed to be a popularity contest," Tom avowed.

"But knocking a man down to size is nothing compared to dethroning his gods," I bellowed.

"Truth isn't a velvet glove, but an iron fist," Tom revealed. "It's on the road to Damascus[230], not Shangri-La, that opens a man's eyes to the world at large. And, as all universal truths, they're to be discovered, not created by man."

"Suicide is still suicide, whether fast or slow," I maintained.

"Truth doesn't care whose toes it steps on in closets, courtrooms or churches," Tom imposed his final will and testimony.

"Don't forget, you're talking about disturbing sleep walkers who not only believe in Heaven and Hell, but place bets upon it every Sunday," I apprised.

"There are inherent risks involved for all cup bearers and messengers," Tom forewarned. "Gods, as tyrants, are meant to be unseated, but man still survived when the gods of Olympus were evicted. Let that be your lodestar[231] when you have reservations and doubts about ends being beginnings."

"Like I said, this is a lot to swallow and digest," I espoused. "Here I find the killers of my best friend and they turn out to be aliens. Not aliens from Mexico, but outer space. That, in and of itself, without anything else, is a lot to process and wrap my head around. Don't get me wrong; I enjoy truth and where it leads me. Most people, however, don't share my commitments and sentiments about life in general or their gods in particular."

"Unfortunately, Mr. Moore, there are no easy open instructions on any can of worms," Tom contended. "Enlightening people is not a mission to be entered into half heartedly because, generally speaking, it's a thankless task that forsakes sanity for another kind of piece of mind. But just as the father must know his children, the children must also know their father. We, more than anybody, know things will not happen and change overnight. There is no such thing as instant success. Instant potatoes perhaps, but instant success? That's a bird of a whole other feather. Always know this: you will never be alone in your ministry out there. You are only the last link in a thirty thousand year old chain of events. And if, by chance, you become hesitant to cast the first stone at glass houses than be the unseen puppeteer behind the scenes who gives animation and words to a perennial stiff."

"Like Madam Curie," Dick wryly noted, "I was the one who put the uranium enriched samples next to that roll of undeveloped film in her dresser drawer."

"Don't get me wrong, it's not that I don't condone or appreciate the truth, it's just that some things should never be let loose and sicced upon the public," I admitted.

"You're forgetting that people and ignorance are never a good match," Tom intimated. "A need to know basis only inhibits the flow of information, bottle necking truth for a select few to sample and savor at their diabolical disposal."

"I hate to sound stupid or anything, but why don't you just tell NASA who you are when you're up there in the safety of Magellan 7?" I stabbed the ceiling as some devil's advocate.

"The main frame that controls all navigational systems aboard Magellan 7 has an override capacity built into its program so Mission Control can commandeer and take over the ship at any time. We will not be safe until we reach the heliosheathe[232] beyond Charon[233], but after the terminator shock," Tom concluded. "We will be in dead space beyond radio contact."

"I guess it's just a lot easier to make me an accomplice to the murder of God and human history," I reluctantly swallowed a pill never found over the counter.

"After the fact," Tom quickly elucidated.

"Before, after, it's the same damn thing," I exacted.

"Only more kinks for you to work out. Just think of it as a work in progress," Tom reassured.

"Which, I suppose, also includes the truth," I scoffed at the mere suggestion

"Especially the truth," Tom issued the warrant.

"Somehow I knew you were going to say that," I derisively remitted, not sure which leg I had left to stand on.

"Remember, Mr. Moore, truth never has one face any more than one voice," Tom educated.

"Yes, but as beautiful as the truth is when she's finally unveiled, she has blemishes too," I retorted.

"You forget flaws alone put the genuine label on leather," Tom tendered.

"But who are electrical prods natural to, ranchers or cattle?" I cross-examined.

"You can never justify food chains, you just come to accept your place in them," Tom briefed.

"Even if it's the truth eating you alive," I tendered.

"You have to ask yourself, Mr. Moore, is it better to perish at the hands of truth or worship at the feet of lies?" Tom hypothetically proposed.

"There has to be a happy medium. There has to!" I decried my sentence.

"I'd like to stay and debate the challenges before you, Mr. Moore, but we have one more master to honor, serve and obey, only this time without gold, frankincense and myrrh," Tom indirectly inferred with a hurried glance at his watch.

"I'm going to have to ask you to move over there," Harry intervened as he motioned to a lumpy sofa stationed on the other side of the room.

Tom then began speaking in a strange foreign tongue I had never heard before. Despite not knowing its etymology and country of origin, I could ascertain a block of instruction was being doled out. The how, what, and why were at the mercy of anybody's guess, but the who held no such debilitating suspense. Then, from a sinister black pouch, Harry effortlessly removed a cylindrical glass vial and menacing hypodermic needle.

"Lay back and try to relax, Mr. Moore," Harry doctorally advised. "You will feel a slight burning sensation before your motor abilities and non-vital organs are shut down. Don't worry—the paralysis is temporary. You will be capable of movement and speech in approximately forty-eight hours."

With a slight push of the plunger, a cloudy, milky substance bubbled from the tip of the shiny needle before suicidally leaping to the shag carpet. The remainder of the pasty fluid was then administered into my bloodstream, where it was soon forwarded to every tingling extremity.

"What if I can't wait five years to tell your tale?" I drunkenly slurred.

"I beseech you," Mr. Moore. "You don't want to know what we are capable of doing to your planet," Tom cryptically warned. We will fulfill NASA's mission regardless of the fact that it's over nine hundred million miles out of our way. All we ask in return is for you to tell the world our story.

"Leave us now," Tom ordered his younger siblings, who promptly exited the foggy den that was gradually beginning to spin like a merry-go-round. "You said you wanted something a little more tangible, something that couldn't be reputed, disputed or called into question. I'm going to grant your wish, Mr. Moore. Just think of it as my going away present from me to you."

Tom then proceeded to my computer where he dutifully began to hammer away at my keyboard, sculpting models, maps, diagrams, and other esoteric, scientific configurations. Screen after screen of runic characters and alien symbols suddenly appeared and disappeared. I had never seen so many continuous, complex mathematical equations and arrangements. I have never seen hands move with such blinding speed and dexterity before. It was an amazing sight, despite the setting and conditions.

Upon installation of a firewall, Tom again approached me, as I lie comatose on the mushy sofa.

"Dying of old age is related more to fear than good genes. When man understands millenniums as moments he will then be considered a student of the Universe. It is your job as our last disciple, Mr. Moore, to give our children that opportunity, that chance," Tom gently patted my numb shoulder after placing the golden disc on the table next to me. He then hurriedly turned to join Dick and Harry in the dimly lit hallway where they soon vanished into the cricketed night and those heavenly skies that held their pin prick dreams.

CHAPTER TEN

One Way Ticket Home

NEEDLESS TO SAY, my life was forever changed after that night. To think everything we learned in school was a master plan by three homesick beings from another world. How could I ever get that out of my head? Everything I knew, everything I believed was all an elaborate hoax to get three wayward sons back home again.

But if knowledge was power, what did that make truth? Was it also a great emancipator? A great equalizer to level playing fields? Or was it only another black hole that ate everything, including light?

Keeping one step ahead of my dilemma was tenuous at best and that incorporated those best of times when model behavior was given free reign of catwalks on the Seine[234]. But between promises and busted cherries, lie bodies in perpetual motion that never know die, not even after sudden death over time. Yet even in the midst of straight dope and Gospel-speak, there was a world buried inside a world man never knew existed during his couponed forays and five-finger[235] discounts.

Is there ever a right time for controversy or for toppling Ivy Towers and other Pyramid Schemes, or even for killing Jesus one more time? Such is my challenge, of which institutions, bridges and stairways to torch first. However, unleashing any eight-hundred pound gorilla has adverse side effects even when it doesn't concern a woman's age, weight and dress size.

After all, telling the truth is very different from hearing it. The chasm is as pronounced as that found when playing music and facing it. The one gets you into deep shit while the other keeps you there without any prospects of ever smelling like a rose again.

You don't know how I struggled with my sanity and a secret that would put all others to shame. The debate forever raged within my soul. Should I personally flip the switch or should I safely pull drawstrings from the distance? I guess perspective in time and space determines how you view anything. All else is open to suggestion, you know, of how one feels in relation to shoes, buckets, and seating arrangements in coach.

How I wish this were an elementary problem that I could simply add, subtract and carry a tiny juvenile over. Everything, however, seems wanting, even when it advertises the same entrées for Last Suppers and potluck dinners. But falling off bandwagons and through trapdoors does tend to gather the same morbid spectators and ambulance chasers.

Why, you ask, did I honor their request? In some ways, even that's an ongoing mystery. I did, however, sympathize with their plight. For the longest time, I was also in a state of shock and disbelief. Who could imagine an alien encounter of the Third Kind in his own home? Mainly, it was those ominous words Tom said to me that night about what they were capable of doing to our planet. That always was in the back of my mind—how could it not be?

My situation was not one of going to sleep and waking up in the dawn of a New Age. This is an ongoing hardship that has no friendly ports to rest my weary head. I interrogated myself for the longest time. Did it really matter who discovered fire, the wheel, computers or nuclear energy? What would it change other than the historical record? It was always a battle between construction and deconstruction, of which bastard son to release next into the Mainstream Media.

My flight home coincides with that night five years ago when Tom, Dick and Harry gave me gifts and secrets to other worlds, including the location of Atlantis and the cure for cancer. It's still madness, however I look at it. I mean, here are Joe's killers giving me the magic bullet to slay the killer of my parents.

Still, there are many questions that need be raised. How can I poke holes in the Social Fabric and still handicap daily rat races with their 9-to-5 long odds? But even when there's a high road to Hell there's still no end in sight. Who knows, maybe illusion is to keep us alive in death too?

In many ways, it's still a guessing game of which tail to pin on unsuspecting asses. That, though, is the damnation when holding skeleton keys to buried treasures. But being the one with coffin nails is like being the doomed navigator on the Flying Dutchman[236], only Judgment Day is a lot closer at hand, not only for me, but for every man.

Above all else I know I have to be careful of labels, for the ones that stick have a tendency of sticking to everything you do or ever will again. There are, after all, no return engagements with first impressions. Once you're exiled to the *National Enquirer*, there's no way to recapture the front page of the *New York Times*. Besides, how do you say, "Oh, by the way, God is dead," while mentioning Tom, Dick and Harry are aliens from another world in the same breath?

There's no turning back now. A promise is a promise, and a man who can't keep his word can't keep much of anything else. Besides, the wheels have already been set in motion with their doctoral hounds[237]. All that remains now is when to set that other archaeological hunt into motion and which Nobel Prize winning scientists to secretly contact?

When you think about it, it's really just a changing of the guard. Man's pursuits will still be the same as will his inevitable final result. All that's basically changed is the Helicon Source[238] from which sprang the Fountains of Aganippe[239] and Hippocrene[240]. And although Tom, Dick, Harry and I never had Paris, we at least came close, if not in that romantic sense, then in that geographic one.

EPILOGUE

Clermont-Ferrand, France

A JOINT FRANCO-AMERICAN ARCHAEOLOGICAL team working on an anonymous tip has unearthed an alien spaceship similar in structure and design to Magellan 7 with nine humanoid skeletons in its burned out hull, officials said Friday. The discovery site near the south central city of Auvergne was today confirmed by Carbon 14 dating[241] to be between thirty and thirty-two thousand years old. Excavation of the surrounding area, noted for its Upper Paleolithic cave drawings, has retrieved more than six-thousand artifacts, the most impressive being a metallic like helmet similar in molecular composition to that employed by NASA on its Magellan Series Rockets. Survey of the crash site and impact crater will continue into the fall.

AP UPI REUTERS
9-13-25

GLOSSARY

1. Brahmin—a cultured person from the upper class
2. "From Hell"—Jack the Ripper signed his letter this way
3. Charlatans—phonies, imposters
4. Right stuff—term for astronauts with the goods
5. Rent—hole, divide, tear
6. Doubting Thomas—referring to Thomas the Apostle, a disciple who doubted Jesus' resurrection and needed to see and feel Jesus' wounds before believing
7. Raising the dead—Viagra
8. Patrician—nobel birth
9. Halycon days—tranquil, happy, idyllic days
10. Dogwager—an elderly woman who is wealthy or holds a high title
11. Dodge—game, trick
12. Iditarod—famous sled race covering 1,150 miles
13. Sierra-Charlie—phonetic alphabet for the letters S-C, which in slang mean to "shit can", to throw away
14. Swirling vultures—helicopters
15. Charlotte Corday—woman who killed Marat in his bath
16. Mitochondrial DNA—structures within eukaryotic cells that convert the energy from food into a form that cells can use
17. Quantico—FBI training center
18. Zodiac Killer—killer in San Francisco circa 1970
19. Devil's Workshop—idleness
20. Depth charge—coffins
21. Chivas—scotch

22. Doggerel—bad, awkward verse
23. Misogynist—hater of women
24. Switch hitter—bi-sexual
25. Ménage a trois—French term meaning the arrangement where three people having sexual relations live together in the same household
26. Hail Columbia—a severe beating or punishment
27. Ivyized—Harvard, Yale
28. Southbys/Christies—auction houses
29. Michelangelo—virus that infected computers in 1990s
30. Neo con—abbreviation for "new conservative"
31. Beyond the pond's reflection—referring to Narcissus
32. Columbian neckties—an execution method that involves a victim's throat being slashed and their tongue is pulled out through the wound
33. Talking heads—T.V. newscasters
34. Aegis—a protective shield
35. Tender mouse—computer mouse
36. Trojan—a condom
37. Unabomber—Ted Kasinski
38. MENSA—I.Q. organization
39. Religious Cookbook—The Bible
40. Empty orchestra—karaoke
41. Plots—graves
42. Deranged countdown of what walks on 4 legs, then 2, then 3—riddle of the sphinx
43. Bowry-a street and a small neighborhood in the southern portion of the New York City borough of Manhattan
44. Potemkin—general in Russian Army who built fake villages to deceive Catherine the Great
45. Scrying—the practice of crystal gazing
46. Cojones—vulgar Spanish word meaning 'testicles'
47. Star chamber—a notorious court in England circa 1641 that ruled arbitrarily, harshly, and without jury
48. Kangaroo court—unauthorized sham legal proceeding
49. Hemp Party—euphemism for hanging

50. Ancient light—a window that can't be obstructed
51. Kotex brigades—feminists
52. Roman Spear—spear of Longines that pierced Christ
53. Monkey wrench—Darwinism
54. 10 speed gears—referring to the 10 commandments
55. Mitred primates—highest ranking bishop in a province; miter is that tall ornamented hat worn by popes, bishops, and abbots
56. Galanty show—shadow puppet show
57. Whitney-Eli Whitney; removable and replaceable parts that he invented for the cotton gin
58. Ad hoc—for this specific purpose, for special case only
59. Dickensian—referring to Charles Dickens; a rough early childhood upbringing
60. Chin music—referring to inside pitch in baseball
61. Flink—a dozen cattle
62. Kuiper belt—area of space debris beyond Pluto
63. Donnybrook—free for all
64. Terminator shock—the boundary between the illuminated and the dark
65. Coalsack of the Southern Cross—most prominent dark nebula in the sky
66. Southern Cross—constellation
67. Camelot-term associated to the Kennedy administration
68. Faustian—referring to Faust
69. Pi—ratio of circumference of a circle
70. Celestial mechanics—science of celestial bodies
71. Mendelian—Gregor Mendel recognized the science of genetics with inherited traits
72. Apple of discord—the golden apple that was the cause of the Trojan War
73. Ophiuchus—constellation between Hercules and Scorpius
74. Draco—7th century B.C. Athenian law giver said be harsh and severe
75. Cheshire—cat
76. Lab rats—lab technicians

77. Loki—Norse god of disorder
78. Ockham's razor—English philosopher who stated that entities are not to be multiplied beyond necessity, that things should be kept as simple as possible
79. Local rags—newspapers
80. Remington—painter/sculptor of Western art
81. Sun City—impoverished city in South Florida
82. Bread trails—money paths
83. 33s on 78—referring to face lifts
84. Gordian knot—Greek myth
85. Lizzie Borden—ax murderer
86. Hesperus—the evening star, Venus
87. Lucifer—Venus at dawn/morning star
88. Augur—an official in ancient Rome who read and interpreted sacrificial blood patterns
89. KEN—range of knowledge
90. 3 hots and a cot—3 meals and a bed in jail
91. The Maine—ship sunk, was the rallying cry for Spanish-American War
92. Gang of fore—referring to golfers
93. Colonel Mustard, Miss Scarlet, Professor Plum—characters from the board game, Clue
94. Doughnut patrol—patrol cops
95. Luddite—Ned Ludd, a destroyer of technology
96. Gambino family—a mob family out of New York
97. Theseus—Greek legend famed for killing the minotaur in the maze
98. Walter Mitty—an ordinary, unassuming man who dreams of being a hero
99. Masonic rub—referring to Masons
100. "Biblibal Jews, who with each successive passing, swelled into a multitude."—referring to Jesus supposedly feeding the multitude with a couple fish and loaves of bread
101. Would-be traveler—referring to Procrustes
102. McCarthy—referring to Senator Joe McCarthy
103. Fighting windmills—referring to Don Quixote

104. Herd of 365—referring to the year
105. Abel bodied victim of the fugitive east of Eden—referring to Cain and Abel
106. Land of Nod—where Cain fled after killing Abel
107. Kasner's childish googolplex-is the number 10^{googol}, i.e. $10^{(10100)}$
108. Mudders—horses that run well in mud
109. Detritus—loose debris, etc.
110. Iroquois Theater—there was a deadly fire at this theater
111. Mystery and abomination—passage in Revelation
112. Square of red and black—checker board
113. Delpic ruins—oracle at Delphi for Apollo
114. Alligator wood—wood burned by extreme heat
115. Ducks and drakes—skipping stones on water
116. White elephant—a possession maintained at a great cost
117. Appellation—nickname
118. ". . . Self portrait hidden in some garret asylum . . ."—Dorian Gray
119. High and tight—crew cut in military
120. Adonis—Greek man noted for beauty
121. Tarantella—a fast, whirling dance
122. Massachusetts mandarin—elite group in New England
123. Urchin—a small boy
124. Fagan—the head criminal in Oliver Twist
125. Anarchists in the marketplace—referring to the Haymarket square in Chicago
126. Quarterly praises—a cuckoo clock chimes every 15 minutes
127. Sirens—in Greek mythology, three dangerous bird-women, portrayed as seductresses who lured nearby sailors with their enchanting music and voices to shipwreck on the rocky coast of their island
128. Snuff films-a motion picture genre that depicts the actual death or murder of a person or people, without the aid of special effects
129. Daguerrotypes—the first publicly announced photographic process

130. Rapidan—river in Virginia where a brutal battle took place during the Civil War
131. Wilderness—battle of the wilderness noted for great loss on both sides
132. Hooker—Union General
133. Grapeshot—a cluster of steel balls fired from a cannon
134. Destroying angels—deadly mushrooms
135. Ephemeral—passing quickly
136. Bloody Kansas—reference to the fighting that took place there
137. Manassas—name of bull run by south
138. Brevet—a novel commission
139. Thrall—slave
140. Stonewall—Stonewall Jackson
141. Swamp fox—nickname of Southern General
142. Bloodiest man in American history—Bill Quantrill
143. Nom de guerre—war name
144. Stygan—dark, foreboding
145. Super liars—referring to prolific crooks
146. Wizards—wise investigators
147. Savant—a man of exceptional learning
148. Bull Run—1st battle of Civil War
149. Andersonville—notorious prison for union soldiers
150. Came, saw, conquered—referring to Caesar
151. Peculiar institution—slavery
152. Hump day—Wednesday
153. Thor's retreat—Thursday, named after Thor
154. Cafe noir—black coffee
155. Lucy—1st woman
156. Pickett's charge—disastrous charge at Gettysburg
157. Idiot box—T.V.
158. Rockoons—rockets launched from balloons
159. Old Sparky—famous electric chair in Florida
160. Memento mori—a keepsake
161. Dewey—decimal system utilized in libraries
162. Calpe—ancient name of the Rock of Gibraltar
163. Jebel Musa—mountain in North Morocco opposite Gibraltar

164. Labyrinth—maze
165. Aides de camp—assistants
166. Cold harbors—allusion to the Battle at Cold Harbor
167. Apostile—a note in the margin
168. 4 eyes monitors—hall monitors with glasses
169. Saturn—god who ate disobedient children
170. Draconian—strict laws; named after Draco
171. Nietzschean extremes—named after Nietzsche
172. Anachronism—out of time and place
173. Coup de grace—merciful blow
174. Minie balls—a cone shaped bullet used in the Civil War; it was noted for its destruction
175. Ironclads—civil war ships made of steel
176. Red badges—allusion to Stephen Crane
177. March to the sea—allusion to Sherman
178. Mason-Dixon—the line separating the north and south
179. Little corporal—allusion to Napoleon
180. Nones—the 9th day
181. Ides—the 15th day
182. General McClellan—general during the American Civil War
183. Exponentially—increasing in extra ordinary proportions
184. Hirsute—hairy, shaggy
185. Noxious weed—Biblical reference
186. Trolls—dwarfs living under bridges or in caves
187. Keloid—scar/tissue
188. Crab's claw—a scar
189. Doppelgänger—a person's double
190. Hercules—a large constellation between Ophiuchus and Draco
191. Light year—approximately 6 trillion miles, one parsec
192. Scorpius—alarge constellation between Orpheus and Ara
193. Antares—a super giant red star in Scorpius
194. Parsec—1 light year
195. Ara—constellation between Scorpio and Pavo
196. Croesus—ancient king noted for his great wealth
197. Trepanning—boring holes in the skull
198. Grafting—transplanting tissue

199. Double helix—strands of DNA
200. Atavistic—appearance in a person found in a remote ancestor
201. Lyceum—the grove at Athens where Aristotle taught
202. Gilgamesh—Babylonian legend reputed to be like biblical flood
203. Ad nauseum—to the point of disgust
204. Levant—Eastern Mediterranean basin
205. Maghreb—Northwest Africa including Morocco, Algeria, and Tunisia
206. Jericho—the oldest inhabited city in the world
207. Proselytize—convert
208. Lothario—a rake; a playboy
209. Washed ashore with 1,000 corpses—referring to Homer
210. Democritus—Father of atomism
211. Extrapolation—to propound
212. Pax Romano—Roman law
213. Roman holiday—entertainment acquired at the expense of someone else's suffering
214. Muses—inspiration to poets
215. Zymurgy—the science of wine making
216. Alchemy—before modern science
217. Cathedrals of higher learning—universities
218. Cartesian—referring to Descartes
219. Across the pond—the Atlantic Ocean
220. Terra nova—new land
221. Great White—allusion to sharks
222. Quid pro quo—something for something
223. Kitty Hawk—original place of 1st flight
224. Sea of tranquility—area on the moon
225. Promethus—a Titan whole stole fire from the heavens to give to man
226. Big Three—big three automakers
227. Oppenheimer—oversaw the Manhattan Project
228. Grandfather clauses—an exception that allows an old rule to continue to apply to some existing situations, when a new rule will apply to all future situations

229. Domesticated bulls—a decree from the Pope
230. Road to Damascuz—allusion to St. Paul
231. Lodestar—the North Star, or any star that guides
232. Heliosheathe—extent of sun's power in the solar system
233. Charon—moon of Pluto
234. Seine-river in Paris
235. Five-finger discount—stealing
236. Flying Dutchman—a famous ghost ship
237. Doctoral hounds—scientists
238. Helicon source—Helicon is the home of the muses
239. Aganippe—the name fountain with its base at Mt. Helicon
240. Hippocrene—a fountain on Mt.   Helicon in Greece said to be sacred to the muses
241. Carbon 14 dating—method to measure time